Life of a Savage 2

Romell Tukes

**Lock Down Publications and
Ca$h
Presents**

Life of a Savage 2

A Novel by *Romell Tukes*

Romell Tukes

Lock Down Publications
P.O. Box 944
Stockbridge, Ga 30281
www.lockdownpublications.com

Copyright 2020 Romell Tukes
Life of a Savage 2

Lock Down Publications
Like our page on Facebook: Lock Down Publications @
www.facebook.com/lockdownpublications.ldp
Cover design and layout by: **Dynasty Cover Me**
Book interior design by: **Shawn Walker**
Edited by: **Mia Rucker**

Stay Connected with Us!

Text **LOCKDOWN** to 22828 to stay up-to-date with new releases, sneak peaks, contests and more…

Thank you!

Submission Guideline.

Submit the first three chapters of your completed manuscript to ldpsubmissions@gmail.com, subject line: Your book's title. The manuscript must be in a .doc file and sent as an attachment. Document should be in Times New Roman, double spaced and in size 12 font. Also, provide your synopsis and full contact information. If sending multiple submissions, they must each be in a separate email.

Have a story but no way to send it electronically? You can still submit to LDP/Ca$h Presents. Send in the first three chapters, written or typed, of your completed manuscript to:

LDP: Submissions Dept
P.O. Box 944
Stockbridge, Ga 30281

DO NOT send original manuscript. Must be a duplicate.

Provide your synopsis and a cover letter containing your full contact information.

Thanks for considering LDP and Ca$h Presents.

Acknowledgments

First, I would like to thank Allah for giving me the strength and will power to make it through my trials in life. I stood tall through every time. Shout out to all the readers from the pens to the streets, keep a lookout, more to come. Shout out to Yonkers, NY, we in the building, Smoke Black, CB, Smurf, Fresh, Awall, Dough Boy, YB, Croddy, my Elm, School Street, OBlock, Strip Nigga. My Bronx niggas, Freddie Frillz, Mill Brook PJs, Melly, Hump aka Ro Balla, Monkey, Ra Money, Dru Boogie, Rob Gs, Mighty, BJ, and B Robb, can't forget Domo. My BK niggas, OG Chuck, Filla, Thug, Tom Dog, K, and Rico. Shout to Malik-4, Chi-raq, Heff, and Coon from Boston. Shout BG, Beast, Rugar, Nap, T-Burn, all my Patterson, NJ niggas. Shout Blue from Newark. Free da red, shout out to the whole 914 (area code) and my 205 (area code) B-ham, Alabama niggas on First 48. Shout to my Harlem niggas. Decuse and Swse, my Staten Island niggas Dex and Free, also ED. Lockdown Publications, big shout out. Thank you for everything. The game is ours. RIP to Casper from St. Louis, you know how we was rocking. This one for you, bro, facts, son.

Romell Tukes

Chapter 1

3 Years Later

Savage's life took a turn for the worse, landing him at rock bottom and experiencing the worst time of his young life. The loss of his friends, his wife being shot, and Bama getting arrested made him feel as if he was trapped inside with no doors to exit.

There was one thing he was truly grateful for, and that was the nosy neighbor, Ms. Jackson. She had called the police moments after Lisa was shot inside her home by Killer and his goons, who'd come looking for revenge.

Lisa died in the ambulance on her way to the hospital. The EMS workers tried to save her, but it was too much blood lost. She'd fought to stay alive the life of the seed growing in her womb.

The doctors were able to save the baby before Lisa fell into a coma, leaving her brain dead.

When Savage made it to the hospital and found out what happened, he passed out. When he woke up, Savage started to attack everybody, including the doctors, his guards, and civilians. The doctors had to strap him down and sedate him.

***

With the help of the crooked DA, witnesses lying and adding shit, and the twelve racist jurors, Bama was shipped off to USP Big Sandy in Inez, Kentucky to do his time in the mountain with Britt's brother, Mice, who'd been down a decade.

Luckily, the two ended up being cellmates, and the best of friends. Mice was a converted Muslim now, so he was heavy on his clean. As for Bama, he was fighting inner demons every day.

Face to face with his harsh life of penitentiary time, Bama struggled with the reality of having to be fenced in behind a huge wall with over 1300 inmates of all races, some of which were never going home and had nothing to lose. It was a battle within a battle, in the prison walls, and in his mind.

Eventually, Bama took a big interest in Islam. It didn't take long before he converted to Islam and focused on becoming a humble Muslim. While being on his clean, he took a step further by teaching himself the Arabic language and became nice at it.

Over time, he'd become so sharp that the inmates made him become the Iman of the prison, because of his knowledge and Arabic skills.

Now with motions in the courts, he was just doing his time and focusing on Allah, while staying away from all the prison politics and bullshit.

***

With a tranquilizer so powerful that he was sleep two days, it took a week for Savage to gather his senses. Savage knew Lisa's life was over, but his wasn't, and the life of his little brother was just starting. That added responsibility brought life back into him.

The city knew there would be a lot of slow singing and flower bringing after that fatal move on Savage's mother. It was inevitable that lives that would be taken, leaving families in mourning.

Detectives arrived at the hospital to question him about the shooting of his mom, as well as the six dead and three injured at his wedding. Savage remained quiet as Sam allowed his legal team to handle all questions, only to frustrate both detectives on the case.

When Savage went to his mom's funeral, that was the hardest part, but he did it with the help of his wife.

Britt was doing well after being shot at her wedding by Killer and almost losing her life on her big day. Savage was right by her side, with his little brother, Abdul aka Lil Smoke, in his arms. He couldn't wait until this phase in his life was over so he could let his mother's soul rest in peace.

***

Three years had passed since Bama blew trial and was sentenced to life in prison. Jada had been in and out of rehab for a while before she pulled herself together, after seeing the lows of her failing life going down the drain.

Jada eventually found a job and then ended up pregnant by her boyfriend, Big Zoe, who was a powerful man in Miami. He controlled the Zoe Pound.

As time passed, and people grew and moved on to a better way of living, Savage bought a mansion in South Miami so his wife and little brother could be safe, happy and have a new beginning as a family.

Sam and Savage still had their business dealings daily. It was the best of both worlds. With Sam supplying Savage with over 300 bricks a week, he was able to take over all of the turfs MPM had before the crew killed all of the top members and ran them out of town.

Now with a bigger and badder crew, Savage was on a new level, and Miami respected his name.

Killer hadn't been seen nor heard from in years, leaving many people to think he was dead or in jail, but Savage knew he was amongst them.

Savage wanted him dead with all his power and energy, so he was a dead man walking, and Killer knew it.

Savage hadn't slept at all since the death of his mother three years ago. Savage vowed to himself that he wouldn't even attempt to sleep until he had the blood of Killer on his hands and face.

He also had a couple of major tricks up his sleeve for a couple of Killer's dear friends, but he understood patience was an important element of life, and his plans.

Savage was very proud of Britt for enrolling in college to become a licensed nurse and aim for a better life. Her marriage was a huge part of her new glow, which enhanced her beauty even more. She honestly had everything any woman could ask for now.

Being a full-time mother to Lil Smoke, since Lisa's death, was like a full-time job, but she knew he needed that motherly love, which she gave him hands down.

Britt wasn't to be slept on. She still had blood on her hands and she had no intention on cleaning them. Things were going too good for the love birds, but they wondered how long it would last. The rational answer was simple, only time would tell in the life of a savage.

Chapter 2

The Present
Miami, FL

"No," Savage screamed as he jumped up in another cold sweat. He was wearing nothing but his Gucci boxers. This had become a daily routine since the death of his mother, years ago. He thought about getting help, but he figured it would just take time to go away.

Savage looked around once his vision fully cleared, seeing that he was the only one is his large master bedroom. The room had fur rugs, a fireplace, photos of black activists, and paintings of famous warriors, like Napoleon Bonaparte, Hannibal, and Julius Caesar.

He glanced over at his nightstand. He noticed the time and shook his head.

"Damn! I missed my morning Faj'r prayer," he scolded himself. This was a prayer that he never really missed, so he felt some type of way.

His mind drifted to Britt, making him smile. He was proud of his wife and how for she'd come in life. Britt was a year away from graduating from the University of Miami with degrees in nursing and physiology.

This weekend was very big for Savage, not because he was turning the big 21 years old, but because it was the weekend he would let his father's name and honor rest in peace once and for all. Big Tone, his father, was killed on the day he arrived in this world. It took years for him to figure out who had killed his father, and just so happened, Sam told him everything he needed to know, years ago. Sam was unaware that was the worst mistake he'd ever made.

Savage climbed out of his custom-made California King Size bed to check on his little brother, who was normally sleep at this time. Ms. Jackson was the nanny, she watched over Lil Smoke 24/7, when Savage was around, and when he wasn't around. She was the main reason why he was alive and well. If it wasn't for her fast thinking the night Lisa was murdered, Lil Smoke wouldn't have made it.

Strolling down the long-carpeted hallway in his good slippers and robe to match, he looked at all the family photos in frames hanging on the wall.

"Damn, she wearing the dress, but I don't remember this picture," Savage said, as if he was talking to a second party.

He proceeded to Lil Smoke's bedroom, hearing the loud TV. The sounds of the Power Rangers were blasting on the 42-inch flat screen he had posted on his wall.

"This little nigga want me to whip his ass this morning, blasting that damn TV like he crazy or pay bills around here," Savage said out loud, as he opened the door and walked in. His little brother was kicking in the air, singing "go, go, power rangers" with a pair of red Power Ranger underwear on top of his head, ass naked. As soon as he turned around and saw Savage, he dived in his bed, trying to hide under the covers as if he was sleep.

Savage could do nothing except laugh at the shocked look on Lil Smoke's handsome baby-face.

"I'm sure you're not sleep, Abdul. What did I tell you about wearing your damn underwear on your head?" Savage questioned him, pulling the covers from over his head.

"I'm sorry. I was about to put them on. Then my show came on. But I know underwear are only made to go on my butt, not my head," Lil Smoke said in a kid voice.

"You ready to eat?" Savage asked, smelling food coming from downstairs.

"No, Ms. Jackson already fed me," Lil Smoke replied, laying down as if he was tired all of a sudden.

Savage thought about how early Ms. Jackson gets up, and nodded his head. She always made sure he ate first. Then she would start teaching him.

"Listen, if you can be a good boy today, I'll take you out later. I just have to make some calls and handle some business first," Savage said as Lil Smoke jumped up and down and his eyes grew wider, like the size of an apple. Every time he went somewhere with his brother, he would have the best time and receive new toys.

Savage walked out smiling, knowing today was going to be a long day.

Lil Smoke was the total opposite of his family bloodline. As far as looks and genes, he looked more like his dead father, Rich, who was killed with Lisa by Killer the night of Savage's wedding.

Lil Smoke had light skin, green eyes, long curly hair, and thick eyebrows. He looked as if he was Spanish, instead of African-American.

All of Savage and Britt's friends loved him, and wherever they went, he always got a lot of attention. People would go out of their way to give him compliments. *If only they knew how bad he really was, they would run the other way* was Savage's favorite line.

Savage walked a little further down the hall to see Ms. Jackson's door closed. Her room was next to the hall bathroom.

"I'm glad she fed his bad ass because I'm tired as hell. I thought she was off today," Savage mumbled to himself before knocking on her door.

"Come in," a soft voice shouted out from behind the door.

Savage walked in her room. She was sitting in a chair, reading a newspaper, with her Chanel reading glasses on and her long hair wrapped in a scarf.

The room was a medium size, regular room, with tons of reading books and kid's stuff neatly stacked in certain places of her room, because Lil Smoke was always in there.

"Well good morning, sleepy head," she said, showcasing her perfect smile and set of teeth, putting all toothpaste actors to shame.

"Good morning," Savage stated, looking at her outfit. She had on a pair of jeans and a blouse, but you could see her thick legs sitting down, and her large camel toe.

"Don't worry about Abdul, I got him under control today. You're free to go anywhere. Is he still wearing them underwear on his head?" Ms. Jackson quizzed. Savage nodded with a chuckle. "That damn boy don't listen." Ms. Jackson closed her newspaper and folded it as she stood to her manicured feet to put on her tennis shoes.

"I took care of it, no worries. We're about to go out soon, so if you can get him ready, that's about it. I'll appreciate that," Savage informed her. His eyes roamed over the tight jeans she wore as she turned around and bent over to tie her shoes. The jeans hugged every curve and seemed to be made only for her amazing body, which was killing a lot of much younger women.

"After that, take off. Go enjoy your life," Savage said, exiting the room.

Ms. Jackson couldn't help but smile. Savage was so sweet to her. He was like a son to her. She was in her forties, but her face was flawless and her body gave any video vixen a run for their money any day of the week. Everywhere she went, males young and old lusted for her attention. Even female asked for her secrets. They asked her how she kept a flat stomach, curves, and good long hair, which was all from taking good care of herself.

Although Lisa, wasn't there to thank her for what she did, Savage made sure he did every day. He felt as if he owed her his life, but she didn't accept anything, not even the money he was throwing at her. She loved being a nanny to Lil Smoke. She used to work at a post office for 20 years, until she retired.

***

Savage had moved his family into a beautiful 7,124 square foot luxury home inside a gated community. It had seven bedrooms, five bathrooms, a game room, an indoor and outdoor pool, and a full court basketball gymnasium for him, his boys, and his guards to play ball. He also had a gym in his guesthouse and garage, located behind the house.

Savage walked through the kitchen and into the French doors of his office to attend to his morning business, as he would normally do every morning after breakfast. But it was nine o'clock and breakfast was over at the moment. He thought Britt was cooking, but she was at school. It had been Ms. Jackson working in the kitchen earlier that morning. He made a cup of coffee from his coffee machine, which sat on top of a small table near the bookshelves on the wall. He thought about asking Britt to play dress up later, maybe a teacher and student, which was his favorite role play. She would ride his dick to the moon. They'd fuck all over the office in her private school outfit as he gave orders, like a teacher.

Savage sat his steaming cup of coffee down before taking a seat in the chair behind his cherry oak desk. He grabbed his office phone, kicking his feet up on his desk after dialing Big Art's cell phone number, which he had memorized.

His mind reflected on the plan he'd put together for the weekend.

"As-salaam-Alaikum," Big Art's voice came alive as he answered the phone.

"Wa' Alaikum Salaam. Art, what's good with it, ock? You ain't scream at me in a couple of days, bruh," Savage stated, putting him on speaker on his office phone, while sipping his coffee.

"Cut it out, big homie. If you take your head out your wife's pussy, you would've seen that I got at you yesterday," Art replied with a laugh.

"Tell her that, nigga," Savage stated with a laugh, burning his mouth with the hot coffee.

"You pussy whipped ass nigga, but what's good with you, big bruh," Art asked.

"Same shit, ock. How about yourself?"

"I just left the mosque. I'm on my way to pick up my man, Gangsta Ock. I was telling you about him. He is a live wire but he loyal to the core. His flight should land in less than thirty minutes. He coming from Victorville USP in Cali," Big Art stated. He was on the highway, trying not to get road rage.

"Ight cool, hit me after you done doing what you have to do. Also, go get Lil Snoop for me. He in Miami somewhere. And then meet me at the spot," Savage stated.

"What happened to his car? That little nigga be riding with Draco's and all types of shit. I'll be damned if I get pulled over just because its three black niggas in my fucking truck," Art said.

"I understand but he totaled his car last night, coming out of Club Eleven," Savage stated.

"I'ma get him," Big Art said, hanging up the phone in his ear.

"He better be ready," Savage spoke out loud to no one in particular, talking about Lil Smoke.

Savage ran back upstairs to see Lil Smoke dressed in his Polo sweat suit with a pair of Jordans on his little baby feet.

"Come on, Lil Smoke, let's go before your big sis come back from school on her break and ruin our little trip," Savage told him.

"Okay, can I go to college like my big sis?" Lil Smoke asked with his puppy dog eyes, which he'd learned to master early in the game.

"Yes, you can. You can be anything you want to be in life, so I'ma make sure you go. Now come on so we can head to Chuck E. Cheese and Toy R' Us."

They both left the mansion and hopped in an all-while CLK Benz with tints, ready to enjoy their day. The guards were tailing them in a black Tahoe with tint, five percent of course. They could see out but nobody could see them.

Life had been very hectic, business wise, for Savage. He owned a very busy, big mosque, a hair salon with Britt, and a barbershop, which had a clothing store attached to it. That was enough to drive a nigga crazy. He was also a co-owner of a new restaurant, which he'd gone half on with Big Art.

Therefore, family time had been fucked up lately, and he felt very bad because Lil Smoke loved attention, just like any other child.

Over the past few years, Savage had turned into a full-blown man, and the king of Miami, at the same time. The streets had given him that title, which would only breed more haters and enemies, with more killing.

The two had a ball hanging out with each other. They got back home close to ten o'clock that night, way past Lil Smoke's bedtime. Ms. Jackson and Britt both had a fit.

Romell Tukes

Chapter 3

Overtown, Miami

Big Zoe was in Casino's mom's house at seven o'clock in the morning, listening to him make up lie after lie, for over an hour, about how he had money across town, how he got robbed by a fiend, and how he was waiting on his brother to bring him some money.

Casino was a low level dealer who had been selling drugs for 18 years and still wouldn't have been able to get right, even if El Chapo was to front him a hundred bricks. He owed Big Zoe 40,000 for two bricks he'd gotten on consignment, months ago, and he'd been ducking him ever since.

Casino had a real bad gambling habit, that's why his name was Casino. He was an ugly Haitian, with most of his teeth missing.

"Please, bruh, I swear I didn't gamble your money away. I'll die before I play with your money, Big Zoe. Please let my mama go cuz she ain't got nothing to do with this." It hurt to see his sixty-year-old mother hog-tied, just like him.

His mother was crying, hating her only son. She felt embarrassed as her saggy breasts hung out of her robe.

"My man, Casino, you think you got all the sense in this small world. You don't think I know you out here flossing in a new Lexus coupe? Which is a luxury car, I must say," Big Zoe said to his goons, as they shook their heads while Big Zoe paced the living room floor.

"You out here hitting up all these baller dice games and casinos with my money. I must look sweet to you, my nigga, like a fuck nigga, or like that gay nigga off of the Empire show," Big Zoe said, making his goons laugh, as they held Casino at gunpoint.

"Nah, folk, never that, bruh."

"Then what? Because I'm lost. I'm a fair nigga," Big Zoe said, staring at him.

"I fucked up, but I'ma get your-"

Boom. Boom. Boom. Boom. Big Zoe cut Casino's sentence off with the sound of the cannon blowing his brains on the plastic cover on the couch, and on his mom's face, as she screamed.

Big Zoe emptied the clip in her frail chest, as her body shook like the Holy Ghost was coming out of her.

"Come on. I got real shit to do. Then we gotta take Jada shopping. Then we got a meeting to attend to," Big Zoe said, walking out of the old-fashioned, two-story house that looked like a nigga's grandmom's house on a Sunday, with plastic covering the carpet, card table, chairs, and mattresses.

Big Zoe was the top leader of Zoe Pound. They had the biggest and most dangerous crew in Miami. Them Haitian boys was feared like Jesus pressing a Jew.

***

Big Sandy Penitentiary

Bama sat in his cell on his two-man bunk, reading his Qur'an in peace, while his celly, Mice, was on a visit with his mule bitch. She was bringing in drugs. He just had to kiss the fat, white bitch.

He thought about how far he'd come with his growth as a man since being in federal prison. Bama now went by the name Abdulla. He ran with the Muslims. He was on Muslim time. He refused to be on south time because the down south niggas were all on bullshit.

22

They were stealing, fucking faggots, and crashing with other cars. He didn't have time for that. As long as his paperwork was good, and he never ratted on a nigga, he was okay.

He was now the Imam of the compound, and one of the most intelligent brothers on the compound, besides Musa from Philly. As his mind started to elevate, so did his humbleness and maturity.

He used his time wisely, mainly exercising for two or three hours a day. He stood 6'2" and weighed in at 250 pounds, solid muscle. There were no weights. He used the stairs as a pull-up bar, and he did dips off the top floor rail in the corner. He loved cardio burpees and navy seals. It was a high intense exercise that would tone Big Pun up in Manhattan. Most niggas exercised to stay war ready in case something popped off, like a race riot.

Abdulla looked up from his Qur'an when he heard keys. He was always on point because he kept a big homemade knife on him, which looked like some street shit.

A correctional officer knocked on his door. "You have a legal visit."

"Okay, thank you."

"You're welcome," the C.O. said, and then walked off to finish his rounds.

"What the fuck could Mr. Lawrence want? He could've just emailed me whatever he had to say, with his money hungry ass," he said to himself.

He looked at his G-Shock watch and brushed his teeth. Then he spit in the toilet before flashing. He cleaned the sink, and then got dressed to go down to see the lawyer.

This was the first time his lawyer had come to see him since he'd gotten sentenced. And for him to come all the way to Kentucky, he hoped it was concerning his appeal.

***

Abdulla walked into the visitation room, only to see Mice sitting across from a fat white woman that was over 300 pounds.

He walked past Mice, trying to hold his laugh because the woman looked much bigger in person than she did in her photos. Mice had met her on a dating site months ago.

Abdulla walked over to the private rooms for lawyers and their clients to speak in private.

Mr. Lawrence sat smiling from ear to ear upon seeing him.

Abdulla walked into the room that consisted of a round table, two burgundy plastic chairs, and a camera in the corner on the ceiling.

"Good afternoon, Abdulla," the lawyer said, standing to his feet and greeting him with a smirk.

"Good afternoon, wipe that smirk off your face. I'm sure I'm not your type," Abdulla said jokingly, but serious.

"I see you changed your name since the last time I saw you."

"You mean when I blew trial and was sentenced to life in prison, while you went on a boat trip or golf tournament with my family's money?" Abdulla stated with his own smirk that turned the white man's face beet red.

The smile that Mr. Lawrence once gave off was replaced with a sad frown, knowing he had a strong point.

"I'm sorry about that, Bama. I'm sorry, Abdulla," he quickly corrected himself.

"So what brings you out here in redneck KKK-Ville? Let me guess, family reunion," Abdulla said laughing and making his nervous lawyer loosen his tie. "You could've emailed or set up an attorney call with my counselor," Abdulla said, wanting to know the reason behind his presence.

"I wanted to deliver the news face to face."

"So lay it on me."

"Well, I'm here because of a new law that applies to you, as well as your appeal motions, and it's been approved. Your appeal was granted by the Supreme Court."

Abdulla sat in silence for a couple seconds to allow what Mr. Lawrence dropped on him to really marinate in his brain.

"Mr. Lawrence, excuse my French, my nigga, but are you fucking bullshitting me? Then again, I don't think you would play with your life with a man who gotta spend his life in the BOP, now would you?" he asked the lawyer, who was now scared and breathing extra hard. "So I'ma ask you this one question. What are my chances of freedom and winning this shit?"

"You bet your ass we can. You'll be coming back to Miami for court very soon, so be ready to give this shit back," Mr. Lawrence told him.

Abdulla wanted to jump up with joy, but he would do that on his own personal time. Right now, he would remain calm.

"Oh, by the way," Mr. Lawrence said, catching his full attention.

"Yeah, boss man."

"The arresting agent that took the stand on you at your trial date was fired and arrested for paying three witnesses at your trial to lie on you. He also gave two of the witnesses sexual favors to stick to their lies. This shit was big. It even made the news because there was drugs involved. He got caught with eight keys of coke." Mr. Lawrence revealed everything to Abdulla, surprised he hadn't heard about the big crooked cop ring bust.

"Naw. Thank you, Mr. Lawrence."

"No problem, you deserve it."

"You know why I was given a second chance, Mr. Lawrence?" he asked the lawyer, who was trying to gather his shit so he could catch his flight.

"Why?"

"Because I had faith. That's all we need. I guess I'll be seeing you in Miami," Abdulla said as he stood to leave, giving him a firm handshake.

After his visit, he went back to his crazy loud unit and prepared for his Asr afternoon prayer with his celly, who was also back from his visit, wanting to shit out his loony full of dope.

***

Big Zoe and Jada were doing some shopping in the mall, but mainly it was her doing all the shopping. Jada hit every designer store on each floor. Big Zoe's goons had already made two trips to the parking lot, filling up the trunks.

"Baby, let's hit the Gucci store. They got this new dress I want that I saw online," Jada said, coming out of the Chanel store with two bags in her hand.

"Damn," he said.

"Damn what, daddy? I thought you said today was my day," she said, poking her thick lips out.

"We just left the Prada department, the Fendi store, and now the Chanel store. Your ass ain't tired by now?" Big Zoe scoffed as he stopped to buy a bottle of water for him and her, from a water stand, in the middle of the second floor.

"No, nigga, I'm not tired. You the only one, Pockie and Rich ain't tired yet," she said, looking at two of his fat bodyguards, carrying her bags and wearing all black. They were tired and nearly sweating.

He wished he'd never come, but she begged him. Or else his dick would be in the sandbox tonight, she'd informed him.

"Okay, babe, this will be the last store. I promise. You spoil the fun in shopping," Jada said as her heels clicked on the marble floor. She wore a pink Versace dress that cuffed her ass and held her breast up firmly. With every step, her ass clapped from left to right. Every civilian she passed couldn't help but stare. It had to be fake was what some of them said to their friend, or in their heads.

"I have to attend to one of the clubs tonight," Big Zoe stressed as he walked side by side with his baby's mother, who had him sprung.

Big Zoe owned two clubs in Miami, as well as other businesses, besides being a plug. As they strolled through the mall, Jada saw two familiar faces, causing her heart to speed up. Her pussy juices started to flow, soaking her thongs, at the sight of Savage's sexy ass.

Jada saw them walking in her direction, so she made sure her presence was known. She wanted to pull out her mirror and touch up her makeup, but Big Zoe was on her heels.

"Hi, Savage, oh my god, I haven't seen you in so long. Look at you, Lil Smoke, you got so big, walking now," Jada said, reaching out to hug him. She held him tightly, and then she hugged Lil Smoke.

"It's good to see you, Jada. How's life treating you? You look clean and like you're doing well for yourself," Savage said, eyeing her in amazement and seeing how thick she'd gotten, and how good she was looking. The last time he'd seen her was two years ago. She was fresh out of rehab, looking crazy.

"Things are good."

"That's what's up."

"I want to thank you for the job you gave me when I came home. I just recently had a seed, a few months ago, and got married," Jada informed him, while looking at Lil Smoke, who was staring at her breasts.

"Hi cutie," she said to him, making Lil Smoke blush.

"That's good, I'm happy for you," Savage said, looking behind her to see a big, black, ugly nigga staring at him with an ice grill. He had some big Haitian niggas with him, who looked like his guards.

"Thanks," she said, not sounding so happy.

"Stay on the right path Allah has chosen for you," Savage said, giving off a sincere smile.

Jada was so caught up in Savage, lusting over him, she totally forgot about Big Zoe's fat ass behind her, staring a hole into her back.

"Oh, this is my baby father over here. I almost forgot," she said with a smile, letting him know he was nothing serious, just her check.

Savage was wondering who the niggas were that were posted, waiting on her, ready to kill him with their eyes.

He didn't want to go over there, but she grabbed his hand, almost pulling his arms off. She took Lil Smoke's hand also, walking them over to Big Zoe, who was standing twenty feet away, next to Footlocker.

"Babe, this my family and friend, Savage, and his son. We grew up together," Jada said, telling a small lie, but Savage caught on to it. Everybody knew Savage didn't have kids.

"It's finally nice to meet you, Savage. I'm Big Zoe from North Miami. I run the Zoe Pound. I heard a lot about you from a close friend. It's my pleasure, bruh," Big Zoe informed him as the two shook hands.

"And who might the close friend be?" Savage asked, not really feeling Big Zoe's vibe. It seemed very fake. It was the type of vibe a nigga gave another nigga who wanted him to stay away from his bitch.

"Mr. New York, I'm sure you're familiar with him," Zoe replied.

"Of course," Savage replied.

"He speaks highly of you all the time. That's a good look. He's a good man. Hopefully, somewhere down the line, we can do business," Big Zoe stated.

"If it's in the cards, we'll see how they're dealt out, you dig. It was nice meeting you," Savage said with a fake smile.

"Likewise, bruh."

"Jada, good to see you again. Take care. We have to go," Savage said, walking off with his brother, not liking the energy. He could tell Jada picked up on it.

He left the mall, wishing he hadn't seen Jada. He couldn't lie, she was looking like a snack with a shake.

Savage had heard a lot about Big Zoe and his vicious Zoe Pound crew. He'd also heard he was a snake in the grass, and couldn't be trusted at all, especially with what he had planned for their friend, Mr. New York.

Savage read through Big Zoe. He already knew what type of man he was, within two minutes of speaking to him.

On the ride home, he was rethinking his encounter with Big Zoe. He only hoped and prayed that Big Zoe would never cross his path because Jada was a close friend, but he would kill her with him, if he had to.

***

Big Zoe's real name was Marqus. He was born and raised in Miragoane, Haiti, where life was hard for him. His parents were poor and stuck in poverty. Living meal to meal was rough, which caused him to enter the streets, where he would rob, steal, and kill, just for a meal.

Big Zoe's family moved to the states when he was a teenager. He went to school, got educated, and tried his best to fit in with the other kids. His parents both eventually found good jobs, which started a better life in a middle class neighborhood.

After he graduated high school, he went to college at Florida State. He majored in science and business management, and received his degrees at twenty.

What most people didn't know about Big Zoe was that he was a borderline genius, but the streets vacuum warped his mind.

Instead of becoming a legit corporate business owner, he used his mind to form a gang of killers and robbers, who moved at his demands.

He studied the 33 strategies of war. He was a mastermind of mind games. He formed the Zoe Pound from the ground up. His partner, Maa, had been killed years ago by him because he thought Maa was getting too much off of what he'd built.

With the disappearance of powerful drug dealers, the Zoe Pound had taken over. Only whispers could be heard about who was behind the disappearance of the dealers.

At the age of 25, he was already a millionaire. The clown part of it was it couldn't bring back his parents, who both died in a car crash on his 26th birthday.

Big Zoe had met New York over 10 years ago in a club called Club Play. Both men were highly aware of each other's status in the street, so it was respect.

Big Zoe and the Zoe pound were new around that time, but making a lot of noise. Back then, it was more about money than violence. Big Zoe just understood that to get respect, he had to earn it, and he did.

New York took Big Zoe under his wing and showed him how to get money and sell drugs the smart way.

Big Zoe put his guns up for a suit and 100 keys and never looked back, once New York showed him the game.

As time went on, the two formed a very close relationship. It was like the bond of a father and son. But unbeknownst to Big Zoe, New York needed him and his team more than Big Zoe and his team needed him.

New York was a successful connect, who sold bricks to the whole south, thanks to his connection with the cartels. Big Zoe was his only muscle. He didn't believe in friends because a friend will cross you faster than your enemy.

New York was far from pussy. He was a killer, also. But if he had to get down or lay down Philly style, then he was laying down on his stomach.

Now it was more about respect than business with these two men. That was why they had a strong liking for each other.

Romell Tukes

Chapter 4

Big Art was on his way to the Miami airport to pick up his comrade and ex-cellmate, Gangsta Ock, who was a very close friend.

There wasn't too many people he could call a true friend, but Gangsta Ock was one of them. On the times when he couldn't make it to commissary, Gangsta Ock gave half of his whole commissary buy to him, and never asked for nothing back.

They'd built a real friendship over the years they spent with each other, never changing up on each other, and remaining solid.

Big Art pulled up in his new BMW truck he'd just purchased two days ago. The airport entrance was crowded as people rushed to go home or catch their flights to wherever.

"I hope this wild nigga changed because it's not the 90's no more," Big Art said out loud as Jay-Z's album blasted in his speakers.

He was looking out his passenger window to see if Gangsta Ock was somewhere in the crowd. It wouldn't be hard to spot him, he was a big nigga with a beard.

Cars were waiting behind him because he was parked in a fire zone with is hazards on, as if it was legal.

When he finally saw Gangsta Ock exiting the airport, he shook his head. He couldn't believe what he was seeing.

"What the fuck is this nigga wearing? I gotta get this nigga to the Gucci store." Big Art laughed to himself. Seeing Gangsta Ock was lost, he blew the horn twice to get his attention because he was really burnt out.

Gangsta Ock looked to his left, once he heard someone blowing the horn. When he saw the black BMW truck parked in the fire zone, he knew who it was.

Once at the truck, he opened the back door, tossing his bag in the back seat. He couldn't help but wonder why his friend was staring at him oddly.

"As-Salaam Alaikum," Gangsta Ock said.

"Wa Alaikum Salaam."

"What's good with you?" Gangsta Ock quizzed as he gave his friends some dap.

"Man, fuck all that shit. Where did you get that wife beater from, homie?" Big Art asked.

"What you mean?"

"That shit been out of style. Nobody rocking a 50 cent tank top, nigga," Big Art said pulling off from the curb.

"Man, whatever. Damn it feel good to be home," Gangsta Ock laughed, looking at all the beautiful women in the parking lot, who were showing a lot of skin. That was new to him because he was so used to seeing female C.O.s in blue uniforms.

"I see you lost weight since we was in Pollock USP. I guess doing pull-ups from off a mop stick was your highlights," Gangsta Ock said as he began to flex his chest muscles.

Gangsta Ock and Big Art had spent years exercising in the pen. It was their life, and what kept them on point.

While most niggas were out there smoking cleave and sniffing dope, they were focus on their mind, body, and soul.

"I see you still got it, big homie, but the only thing I need to work out is my eyes and trigger finger, nigga. I know for a fact niggas ain't fighting or wrestling in the streets," Big Art said, pulling out a desert eagle from under his seat.

"This shit going to take all the fight out of a nigga, believe that shit," Big Art said, laughing and placing the gun in his lap.

"Yea, you right."

"You know this not the 90s no more. Niggas can't take a ass whipping no more," Big Art said, driving down the expressway.

"I just did a 15-year bid, homie, and 12 ½ out of that, so the only trigger I'ma be pulling is a clit on some bitch pussy," Gangsta Ock said, not trying to go back this time.

"I feel you, bruh. I dig that shit, but do you like this truck? I know how you used to always talk about it," Big Art asked as he accelerated, showing off the speed on the empty highway, by-passing a couple of cars.

"Hell yeah, this some shit off a car magazine. and I like how you stole my dream car, black truck, peanut butter seats, and a little surround sound," Gangsta Ock said.

"Man, you always talking before you think. This is all you, nigga. Welcome home. You crash it, then I can't help you," Big Art revealed as he watched the smile creep across Gangsta Ock's big face.

"Damn, ock."

"Damn what? This ain't shit, trust me."

"Thank you, bro. This is a blessing from Allah," Gangsta Ock humbly stated.

"It's nothing. I owe you more. You saved my life in the pen," Art said, thinking back to the race riot that popped off in the yard. A Mexican had almost taken his head off from behind as he was putting in work, but Gangsta Ock crushed the Mexican.

"Bruh, as I told you before, you don't owe me shit."

"Yeah, I know. But we still family, and family look out for each other," Big Art said, getting off Exit 6.

"No doubt, big boy, but I have to check with my P.O. to see if it's cool to drive. I gotta see what she on. I'll be damn if I'm one of them niggas that left and came right back twenty days later," Gangsta Ock stated, thinking about a lot of niggas he'd met that came right back.

Big Art shook his head in full agreement, "I have a few more surprises for you. Just know you're family now, Ahkee, and I have a family I'm a part of, which makes you a part of us," Big Art said.

Gangsta Ock wondered what he meant.

"We've built a strong brotherhood in Miami, but we're all bonded by Allah and loyalty. So I'ma take you to meet the family. A lot has changed since you been away, and believe me, a lot, ock." Art schooled him as Gangsta Ock listened, knowing Art was like a real blood brother to him, who wouldn't lead him astray.

They'd held each other down since day one. They were together in Pollock USP and Hazelton USP where they were in gang wars, riots against the Aryan Brotherhood, Mexicans and even fights against their own Muslim brothers, who were on D.C. time.

No matter what, they were true to their religion, and each other. What was understood didn't have to be said between them.

***

Justin Robinson Jr, aka Gangsta Ock, grew up in the Northeast section of D.C. where you were either getting money, killing, or robbing just to survive on the streets. Gangsta had caught his third body at an early age. Life had been hard for Gangsta. The streets named him Gangsta, but in jail he change it to Gangsta Ock, after learning his Islamic clean, and practicing it because he was born a Muslim.

Growing up in a single parent home was a strain on his mother. His father was sentenced to 225 years in prison for two murders of federal agents, who didn't identify themselves during a robbery he'd committed. Although that didn't save him from a guilty verdict, it saved him from the death penalty. With his mom left to raise a fatherless child on her own, she turned to crack, which only led her to sell pussy to any nigga willing to pay so she could support her high, and maybe pay a bill or two.

Growing up in D.C. alone was crazy, he just become another black man claimed by the D.C. streets. If you asked him who his mother was, he would be quick to say "Northeast Slim." It made him calculated and cold-hearted.

After his first baby at the young age of sixteen, his reputation grew, and he received the handle Gangsta. At the age of 18, he was able to buy his mom a house, cars, and jewelry, which all came from the hands of murder victims, robberies, and drug selling.

Gangsta was way ahead of his time in D.C. Just as everything seemed to be going right, his life quickly took a turn for the worse.

One night, Gangsta Ock was coming home from a downtown club in his new Lexus coupe. Upon passing a project he was beefing with over some pussy, he noticed a familiar face.

Gangsta saw the man who'd murdered his friend, Goose, a few weeks prior, in broad daylight, on Alabama Ave. Without hesitation, he pulled up and jumped out of his car with his gun clutched in his hand and one thing branded in his mind, murder.

Gangsta Ock ran down on the group of niggas posted up in front of the building with the kid. He started shooting like a madman, killing the kid with a headshot

Unbeknownst to Gangsta Ock, a police cruiser MTA was parked around the corner on a stake out. The officer saw everything. Even though the streetlights were dim and it was a dark area, they still saw the crime. They tried to make the arrest, but Gangsta Ock took flight.

He tossed the murder weapon in a garbage dumpster. Luckily, trash day was the following day. He figured the gun could never be found.

Gangsta ran through backyards and people's homes, leading the cops on an hour-long manhunt through the city before he was captured.

Once he got sentenced to 15 years on a plea deal, he spent massive time studying his belief, Islam, and becoming a better person.

***

Hours later after, the men went shopping at a designer outlet on Collins Ave, Big Art took Gangsta Ock to his new apartment, which made him happy because he'd never had his own place.

Then it was time to meet the family. They made their way to North Miami. Once in Carol City, Big Art went to pick up Lil Snoop, who was quiet on the ride to the meeting because he had no clue who the nigga in the passenger seat was.

Once at the closed soul food restaurant which Big Art partly owned, he led the men into the basement where their meetings were normally held.

"First and foremost, I would like to greet and welcome our new family member and brother, Gangsta Ock. As-Salaam Alaikum," Savage said, greeting him with a hug and smile.

"Wa Alaikum Salaam, man, I heard a lot about you in the pen. Them MPM niggas was talking about you daily," Gangsta Ock said, having no clue Art was dealing with a man he'd heard so many stories about.

"I hate them niggas, but welcome home. This is Lil Shooter and Lil Snoop," Savage said as both of them gave him dap.

"Today is a big day, fellas. I've been planning this day for years, gentlemen, so let's be focused and on point. One slip can be deadly," Savage said, looking around the round table. "We about to take down the biggest supplier in Miami. We have one hour to make our move. Everybody will have positions, even you, Gangsta," he said, looking at Gangsta Ock, who looked a little confused. It was his first day home, he wanted some pussy. He had 72 hours to report, and he was about to kill in less than 24 hours home.

"We will kill every soul in there. You know my motto, no witness, no case," Savage continued, looking at Lil Snoop smiling and dressed in all black, ready to put in work.

I know how to get past security, in and out. Their guards are totally down when it comes to me. They don't search me or nothing, because they see me daily.

"It's like taking candy from a baby gorilla," Big Art said.

"Gangsta Ock, I want you in front, laying shit down, while Lil Shooter and Lil Snoop cover you trying to get in, because all the guards are mainly in the front.

Once Lil Shooter heard he had to cover for the new nigga, that touched a nerve, and Savage could tell. But he knew Gangsta Ock was more experienced than both of them in the battlefield. He was a thinker and they were shooters.

"Big Art, you rolling with me, but you coming through the back yard where the woods have a trail leading to a highway. It's like two miles away. I'ma have another team on standby for back up, but this will be the element of surprise, so Inshallah we can come out on top," Savage expressed with a smirk.

Savage stood up and questioned everyone about being ready, and all he heard were the sounds of four guns cocking as their final answer to his question.

"Then let's ride on these niggas," Savage said, picking up his Draco leading his crew out the door.

Chapter 5

An hour later, Sam, aka New York, was in his mansion, getting himself ready for his business trip to Atlanta to meet with a very powerful man to discuss some new business plans. Sam stood in his master bedroom admiring his chiseled body in his large mirror attached to his walk-in closet door. He was in his 40s but when he pulled of his shirt and cut all the grays out of his beard, everyone thought he was still in his early twenties.

Five days a week, he made sure he spent two hours in the gym in his garage, which had almost every type of workout equipment you could find Gold's Gym.

"Damn, I still look twenty," he spoke to himself as he rubbed his abs, which felt like blocks, and stared in the mirror, smiling. Then he heard a loud boom.

Sam ran to the TV monitors on his wall, where cameras showing the inside and outside of his property were located.

The cameras were all completely out.

"Tiny, what the fuck is going on?" New York shouted towards downstairs, trying to get the head of security's attention. When he didn't get a response, he grabbed his assault rifle from under his bed and exited his room.

***

Downstairs, Savage was stepping over dead bodies that he and Lil Snoop put down with their guns, which has silencers, as well as extendos, attached.

Savage entered the gates easily. He claimed he had a meeting with New York, so they let him in. Security was thinking it was a regular meeting with the boss.

As soon as he exited the truck, he started taking guards out, while Big Art entered the back and took out the power to make it look like a blackout. It was ten o'clock at night, so it was already dark outside.

Gangsta Ock and Lil Shooter came through the front door, guns still smoking. There were eleven dead guards outside. Boom. Boom. Boom. Boom. Boom. Boom. Boom. There were guards in the house going bullet for bullet with the crew, in the dark.

"Go left, we going to take the right," Savage told his crew as they went separate ways. Gangsta and Lil Shooter took out three guards as they ran down on them from behind, hitting them in their faces and necks.

Savage dodged two bullets coming his way at the speed of sound.

"Damn," Savage said. He leaned on the side of a wall as the bullets took huge chunks off the wall.

Lil Snoop saw he had a good shot on both men and he took it, hitting both men directly in their heads.

"I believe we killed the whole security team," Lil Shooter stated as the gunfire paused.

"Let's count the bodies later. We not done, but where the fuck is Big Art?" Savage said, looking around and seeing only his crew standing, surrounded by dead bodies lying in puddles of blood.

Big Art came out from the back with a perplexed expression on his face.

"What the fuck is wrong with you, and why you got that damn look on your face?" Gangsta Ock quizzed him, knowing something was wrong with his friend.

"I just killed two badass white bitches. They hopped out the cabinet on me in bikinis. You should've seen that shit. Oh and a old lady with a shotgun, the bitch almost blew my fucking head off," Big Art said, shaking his head in pure disappointment as he approached them.

Everybody was laughing until bullets started flying everywhere from a powerful assault rifle being fired from upstairs. Everyone was ducking trying to take cover to prevent from being shot by the last man standing, their main target.

***

New York's mansion was huge, especially on the second floor. There were so many rooms that a nigga could play hide and seek.

Sam ran from door to door upstairs, as he let off shots at the gunmen. He thought he had them when he saw them laughing, taking a break.

"Y'all done fucked with the wrong gangsta," he shouted, letting off shots from his assault rifle. He was ducking back behind room doors because Savage and his crew was busting back, round for round.

Savage saw an opportunity to block New York in, as he looked at Big Art, who was on the other side near the staircase.

Once the shooting slowed down Savage pointed two fingers towards the top of the steps, and both men made their move, as if they were on the special op team about to move on a known terrorist.

New York was trying to reload his 50-round clip, but he was so nervous his hand was shaking like a stripper and the clip fell on the ground.

As soon as he bent over to pick it up, he felt the butt of a gun hit him so hard that he dropped his weapon as he fell slumped on the wall, losing his balance. Then he passed out.

Minutes later, he slowly opened his eye, hoping he was just in a dream.

"It's nice of you to finally join us," Big Art said, kicking him in his stomach for almost shooting him downstairs.

"Uggh," New York winched in pain.

"Shut the fuck up," Lil Snoop said with his pistol in New York's face.

"What the fuck do you want? The money and drugs are in the vault in the bedroom closet. The code is 2-10-90-1-7," Sam shouted in pain, as if they were robbers.

Lil Shooter and Lil Snoop wasted no time and went to collect their prize, as if they were at a fair.

"I don't want your money, old man."

Once Sam heard the familiar voice, he thought his ears were playing tricks on him. Then he saw Savage appear from behind Big Art and Gangsta Ock, who had him at gunpoint on the floor.

"Surprise," Savage stated as he saw Sam's eyes pop out, like he just saw a ghost.

"What the fuck, Savage? You're making a big mistake, youngin. I never crossed you, and now you come in my home disrespecting me."

Savage couldn't help but laugh.

"I made you, nigga. You come in my home, kill my men. You're a fucking snake," Sam shouted in a loud angry voice.

"Save all the tough talk. This is personal, Sam. You killed my pops, Tone, and fucked up my youth and adulthood. It was very hard growing up without a father. Do you know how that feels?" Savage asked. "Now I'm here for payback, Sam. Karma a bitch, ain't it?" Savage replied with a wicked smile.

Sam's eyes lit up brightly in fear, realizing it was Lil Tone in his presence.

"Savage, that was a long time ago," Sam said.

"Nigga, please cut it out," Big Art said.

"His pops killed my fucking brother. It's the game. But we can put all this behind us and get rich, young blood. Put the gun down, please," Sam pleaded.

"Can we just kill this cry baby? He killing my ears," Gangsta Ock said, leaning on the wall, ready to smoke this nigga and getting tired of his pleads.

"Nah, Ock, this is a special day. Gangsta Ock, go bring the gas and fire, and tell Lil Shooter and Lil Snoop to hurry up. Tell them to load whatever they can. We almost done here," Savage said, putting his attention back on Sam.

Once he left, Savage started pistol whipping Sam so badly that all of his teeth started flying every which way.

Big Art couldn't watch, seeing the disfiguring of Sam's face right before his eyes.

Savage beat him with his pistol for at least seven minutes straight.

"It's the game, but its Savage life, bitch nigga," Savage yelled as the beast came out of him and he beat Sam until he stopped breathing.

Big Art saw how Savage had blood all over his clothes, face, and hands.

Savage wasn't done just yet. He wanted to make this a night to remember.

He shot Sam in the head eight times before he burned the house down to the ground, on some Left Eye from TLC shit.

***

The next night, Savage was out celebrating his twenty-first birthday with his crew at Club Mansion.

They were all turned up in the VIP section, which was packed with over fifty bottles with sparklers and all types of liquor.

Britt was also there, supporting her husband and watching out for the thirsty bitches, as she enjoyed the scene next to her boo.

Savage wasn't a drinker; he just liked to sit back and watch everyone else get drunk and enjoy themselves.

The club was big packed with one big floor, one bar, disco lights, two VIP sections, bottle girls from all over, who were Instagram famous, and the hottest DJ in the city, killing the booth.

The young boys of the crew, Lil Snoop and Dirty Redd, were out on the dance floor getting busy to the Rick Ross song "BMF" that had the whole club in an uproar.

Britt looked at her husband, noticing the glare in Savage eyes that showed happiness, something she didn't see all the time.

She leaned over to whisper something in his ear, making him smile bright.

"I'm glad we made it, baby. Most young niggas don't make it past sixteen, and you're twenty-one, baby. I'm proud of you," she said.

"That's on everything, it's a cold game," he shouted over the loud music as everybody in the VIP was tipsy and enjoying themselves.

"You're everything a real woman can ask for. Even if we didn't have money, you'll still be the perfect man in my eyes," she said, kissing him while her hand eased on his manhood.

Britt was looking sexy in a real Ralph Lauren dress, with a slit showing her thighs, and a slit from her chest down to her stomach, showing her breasts.

Savage rocked an all-white Hermes outfit that had gold outlining on his pants to match his white and gold Gucci loafers.

She knew exactly what she was doing, making the other women realize they stood no chance to even have a conversation with the King of Miami.

The dance floor was jammed packed and everybody was turned up to the max, until a dark skinned Mavado lookalike pushed Lil Snoop out of his way, causing him to almost fall.

Lil Snoop was 6 feet tall and skinny. He was able to catch his balance, but once he saw the man who pushed him, he smiled.

"Get out my way, little nigga, or next time it will-" Before the dark-skinned man could finish his sentence, Lil Snoop two-pieced him with some fast shit, knocking him clean out.

Once the party goers saw that it was on and popping, a mob of dread heads came from every direction, trying to attack Lil Snoop. But he was too quick and skillful with his hands. That came from years of boxing and kickboxing.

He knocked two more dread-heads out, taking them down one by one as he bopped and weaved, hitting them with all types of combinations.

Dirty Redd was on the other side, dancing with three white females, until he saw Lil Snoop banging out with a gang of Jamaicans, it looked like.

He made his way over to help him. He grabbed one of the men by his dreads and pulled out his pistol. He started pistol whipping him right in the middle of the dance floor.

When his boys saw the gun, they froze as Lil Snoop was stomping two of the men. Guns weren't allowed in the club, so when they saw Dirty Red, they backed down, scared to get shot. Most of the party goers had already taken cover, just in case niggas started shooting again.

Gangsta Ock and Big Art ran to the dance floor with about twenty of Lil Snoop's goons from Jacksonville. They started fucking up every dread-head in the spot.

By the time security cleared the way to the middle of the dance floor where it was going down, most of the patrons had left in fear of their life.

Savage was on his way down there, but it was already over. He was just happy nobody got murdered or shot. On his way back upstairs to his VIP sections with his crew behind him, he saw ten dread-head niggas in suits. He thought it was a joke.

Savage, Britt, and his crew reached for their guns, all at once. Then a loud voice boomed, approaching them from behind.

"It's no need for that. I'm sure you all did enough in my club tonight," Big Zoe said.

Once Savage saw who it was walking behind them, he eased up. It was Jada's boyfriend, who he'd met a couple weeks ago.

Big Zoe was upstairs in his office, watching the whole scene, from beginning to end, on his monitors. He knew who was in the wrong, and who wasn't, but he had no clue it was Savage's crew until he came downstairs and saw him.

The two men locked eyes, like two raging bulls in the wildlife jungle.

"It's good to see you, Savage, considering these fucked up circumstances in my club tonight. But shit happens," Big Zoe stated with a disapproving look on his face.

"I would say the same. But if there is anything I can do to repay for the problem we just caused, then it will be my pleasure. I only come out to have a good time with family and friends," Savage spoke like a true businessman.

Big Zoe's crew was posted behind him, staring at Savage's crew as if they wanted some trouble. But Savage's crew didn't blink, and they loved the taste of blood.

Big Zoe pulled Savage to the side with him, in private, as the other club patrons continued to party and enjoy themselves. Big Zoe's motto was "bosses only talk to bosses."

"Don't worry about the club situation. This shit happens every weekend. I would like to speak to you about our friend Sam," Big Zoe stated, while looking Savage in his eyes.

"What's going on? I heard what happened. That shit touched me," Savage said genuinely.

"He was murdered yesterday, as well as his men. The news reports and police reports say it was gruesome sight."

"I saw it on the news last night."

"They also burned down the man's house. They couldn't even recognize him. They had to use his dental records to identify him," Big Zoe said, looking for any guilt in Savage's face. He saw none. If only he'd known that Savage's poker face game was hardcore.

"He was a like a father to me. He did a lot for me, and he showed me the game. I owe it all to him. I can promise you, I'ma find his killer," Savage said, returning the same look Big Zoe gave him, as if he was the culprit.

"Yeah, I'm on it as we speak. Trust me, it will all come together. He groomed me and showed me the ins and outs to the game, when nobody else would. I owe him a lot, so the least I can do is murder his killer and their whole family when I get wind of who was behind it," Big Zoe said coldly.

"Let me know so I can join. I love the smell of fresh blood. That's on everything," Savage stated.

"Ok, good, but I have business to handle, so please excuse me, and enjoy your night. Order whatever, it's all on the house," Big Zoe said about to walk off.

"Thanks, but I already bought the bar out for the night," Savage said, walking back to the VIP section. His crew was all ready to bounce, so they all left the club.

Savage knew that wouldn't be the last he heard from the Zoe Pound. *Maybe next time it won't be so sweet*, he thought.

Chapter 6

Big Zoe and his crew sat in his spacious office, rethinking the events that had just taken place an hour ago, in his club. "Big Zoe, why you let them niggas go free? Them niggas almost killed us, man. I can't believe this shit," Big Moe said, rubbing his fresh black eye that Lil Snoop had given him. Big Moe was 6'5" tall and 265 pounds of muscle, a gym rat, built like a gorilla. He was one of the security guards. All of Big Zoe's guards and crew were Haitian, or half Haitian and half Cuban, but one could never tell.

Big Zoe gave Big Moe a look that made him sit down. He knew his limits.

"Why don't you shut the fuck up, you big pussy, before I pistol whip you? What the fuck is wrong with you, talking like you the shot caller? Nigga, you just got knocked the fuck out," Big Zoe said, leaning over on his desk.

Everybody in the room laughed because Big Moe acted as if was the hardest killer in the city, so to see him with a black eye was funny.

Big Moe was silent as he sat down. He knew firsthand that Big Zoe meant every word he spoke.

Big Zoe looked towards Zoe Fresh before speaking his capo.

"Something isn't adding up about this little nigga. I got a funny feeling about him that rubs me the wrong way," Big Zoe said with his hand on his chin as he leaned back in his lazy boy leather recliner chair.

"I agree, boss," Charlie said, standing by the office door. He was the oldest of everyone in the room, and still on bullshit. His voice was deep, with a strong Creole flow and accent.

"They have no connect. Why would they be out partying and ballin like there was no tomorrow? The bartenders informed me that they spent close to 200,000 in here today. Now tell me if I'm missing something," Big Zoe questioned.

Nobody said a word because they knew he was just talking out loud, to no one directly.

"Am I tripping, Zoe Fresh?"

Zoe Fresh wasn't much of a talker, so he just slowly nodded his head in agreement. He just wanted to know who his next victim was, so he could have another bloodbath, as he'd done with the Cubans and other rivals.

Most would consider Zoe Fresh a Mad Max from the movie "Shottas." He was Big Zoe's hitman. He always kept him close and tucked, just for times like this.

"I want you to GPS these niggas, and when it's time, it's a go. I ain't playing with these young niggas. For now, just be mindful," Big Zoe stressed as he exited his office.

***

Big Zoe made it home, where he saw Jada sitting in the living room on the couch, staring into the fireplace they had installed.

He snuck up on her from behind, scaring the living shit out of her. It was bad enough he was big and ugly. It was hard for her to even wake up to look at him, and he had the nerve to scare her.

"Boy! You scared the shit out of me. You know you black as hell," Jada said, laughing and holding her chest.

She got up to give her man a hug as her silk robe unraveled, showing her pink and white sexy lingerie, with her ass and breasts busting out.

"Miss you, boo," he said, gripping her fat, soft ass.

"I missed you, too. How was your night, Mr. Marqus?" she asked as they both sat down.

"A little crazy. Your family, Savage, and his crew fucked up my club. It was a big brawl. They put two of my men in the hospital. If it wasn't for you, baby, or Sam, he would have been in someone's lake, swimming with the alligators," Big Zoe said, shaking his head.

Jada just sat there, listening and rubbing his shoulders.

"They would've met their maker tonight," he said, pissed off about how that shit went down.

Jada just nodded her head, though in her mind she knew he was out of his league by fucking with Savage, but she kept it to herself.

Every time she heard or thought of Savage, her pussy got wet. But she knew Savage wasn't too much of a party-goer, so she wondered what he was doing out. Then it hit her, tonight was his 21st birthday.

"Baby, did you hear me?" Big Zoe said trying to bring Jada mind back to reality.

"No, I didn't. What did you say?" Jada asked, looking at him now.

"I said why, outta all the clubs in Miami, he was in mine?" he asked, as if Jada knew.

"It's his birthday, baby," she stated calmly.

"How the fuck do you know that?" Jealousy was evident in his tone.

"I told you I grew up with him. He's family, babe. That's it, damn," Jada responded with an attitude.

"I'm sorry, baby, I got a lot on my mind. You know how I can get when it comes to you. Good pussy can make a nigga go crazy." He chuckled as he continued, "but you know how some girls be always saying a nigga is my friend or family when they really not?" He asked, making a point as his phone was ringing, but he shut it off.

"I'm not every girl, I'm your wife. I don't have to lie to you. I do have male friends I grew up with, just like you have female friends you grew up with," she said.

"I'm sorry I told you," he replied.

"Whatever, nigga," she said, sitting Indian style, exposing her fat pussy as her pussy lips busted out the sides of her thong.

"Where's my son?"

"He's asleep, Marqus, and don't go waking him up. I have a little treat for you anyway." Jada got up, stepped back, and dropped her Givenchy robe.

She placed her left leg on the couch, showcasing her clean shaved plumed pussy, which was dripping wet and fat like a muffin.

Big Zoe slowly inserted two fingers inside of her wetness and played with her.

"Ohh shittt," she moaned as she slowly moved her hips until her legs trembled. She then guided his head to her pussy, and he began to suck on her clit while she went crazy.

Within seconds, her thick, warm, cream filling was all over his face and fingers, but she hadn't even come yet.

Big Zoe and Jada quickly undressed. He laid Jada on the couch and started sucking her swollen clit while fingering her fast at the same time.

"Oh shit, baby, go dddeeper," Jada shouted.

Her shouts and moans instantly started to turn Big Zoe on.

She forced his head deeper into her watery pussy as he ate her box like a snack.

"I-I-I- cumm-mming!" Jada squirted her juices in Big Zoe's mouth.

Big Zoe was eating that shit like a champ, as if he was trying to punish her.

Unbeknownst to Big Zoe, her thoughts were on the man who she lusted over daily. Every time she came, she only thought about one person, Savage.

Big Zoe definitely knew how to eat a bitch's back out. She'd never had her pussy ate the way he did.

That was the only thing he had going for himself, besides a big bag that could last a lifetime.

His dick was the size of a mini Snicker's candy bar when he was hard. The only reason why she married him and gave him a seed was because he had a lot of money and was willing to take care of her when she was at her low points in life.

The only part about sex that she hated was the fucking part because it teased her. She would normally masturbate after, just to get her nut off, because he would fall to sleep very quickly.

She wanted that part to be done and over with. She bent over on the couch with her fat, round, perfect, unblemished ass tooted in the air.

As soon as he slid into her wetness, he moaned. She had the best pussy he'd ever had, straight knock out Mike Tyson.

She started to throw her ass back a little, not so much because he would normally slip out, and then have to find his way back inside of her quickly.

"Oooh god!" Jada screamed as she looked over her shoulder at him, giving him a sex look, as if he was killing her shit.

Big Zoe was sweating on her ass and back, already tired, as he was going to work, or at least he thought he was.

"Yeah, take this dick, bitch. I'm in your stomach." he gritted as she acted along.

"Yesss, Yess, that's my spot, bbbaby, fuck your pussy," Jada yelled as she performed an Oscar-worthy scene, as always.

Ninety seconds in the pussy and Big Zoe's eyes were rolling in the back of his head as he let off a thick load of cum inside of her.

Jada felt him pull out and she felt his nasty cum inside of her.

She didn't even get a chance to cum, but this was daily so she wasn't even mad. Big Zoe fell onto the couch and went out like a light, snoring and grinding his teeth, which were already fucked up.

Jada moved from off the couch, looking down at him and wishing he was Savage.

All she could do was shake her head as she walked to the bathroom to clean herself up. She hated when he sweat on her, but she really hated when he nutted in her.

She always felt dirty after having sex with Big Zoe. After cleaning herself, she went downstairs in the nude to the library in their mini mansion, which had 4 bedrooms, 2 bathrooms, 2 guestrooms, a library, basement, game room, outdoor pool, and a greenhouse where Big Zoe grew weed.

She took a seat behind the small desk where her laptop was sitting and logged in. Big Zoe didn't invade her privacy, and she didn't invade his.

Once on her Facebook page, she search for the person she was looking for while she placed one leg on the desk.

Jada began playing with her pussy looking at Savage's pictures on his Facebook page. This had been an every night thing for years. Once she was done, she licked her fingers, loving the cherry vanilla taste. She texted him "Happy Birthday," and then went upstairs to go to sleep with him and their recent encounter on her mind.

***

It had been a long night of rough, passionate sex with Britt. They'd done everything under the sun, even made up some new shit. Savage made sure he fucked her to sleep, even though she almost made him tap out twice because of her crazy head game.

He was meditating in his quiet room. With so much weight on his shoulders and mind, he needed a peace of mind.

Savage checked his emails on his laptop to see if Bama's lawyer had responded to his last week email asking what the fuck was going on.

He scrolled down his emails to see he had a new one from Mr. Lawrence that read:

In a couple months, Bama. Excuse me. Abdulla, was granted an appeal hearing to be released.

Savage was so happy for his best friend. This was the best news he'd heard in a while. After he logged out, he went onto his Facebook account to post something on his page for his thousands of followers.

He saw he had a message from Jada that said "Happy Birthday," which made him smile. She'd also left her number in his inbox.

He made a mental note to himself to call her and set up a lunch date. Jada was good people, and she'd come so far.

He thought back to when she'd lost her mom and began smoking crack and selling pussy at a young age. He remembered sending her to a rehab, just for her to come out and relapse again, before she finally got it right.

Savage also made a mental note to himself to holla at Lil Snoop about fucking up his B-Day party, but also knowing someone could've lost their life in there.

Everyone in the crew knew Lil Snoop knew how to box, but that shit couldn't stop no bullets. In his field, Savage learned to carry himself as a businessman and gentlemen, not a thug or gangster.

He was the Alpha male and he and had to conduct himself as a good leader for his crew to trust in him.

Savage never wanted to instill fear in any man. The fear of being killed or someone's prey was deadly, even though it was all a part of the game.

One thing that he knew was respect got you ahead of the game in this cold world, but respect, power, and money placed you in a position. Checking the time, it was 4am, so he shut off the computer and went to check on Lil Smoke, who he knew was asleep.

When he walked inside the colorful room, the TV was blasting, as always, making him shaking his head as he turned it down.

"I can't wait for this nigga to get a job," he mumbled to himself, walking out towards his room.

Savage wished his mother was there to witness how smart, witty, and joyful Lil Smoke was already.

Every time he thought about his mom and looked at what his baby brother was missing out on, he got emotional.

Those emotions made his mind think about Killer, whom he'd placed a five-million-dollar bounty on.

Savage prayed every night that Killer would show his face again so he could pay for his mother's life with his.

Chapter 7

Gangsta Ock had a long night, but he'd had a longer night after the club scene. He, Big Art, and a couple of goons had hit up a couple of more of the hottest clubs in Miami. Most of the hot clubs were located on South Beach Blvd. It was a long strip of bars and clubs, full of every race known to men.

After the club, they went to the Waffle House in South Miami, where they met a couple of chicks that were fresh out of a club, looking for the after party.

Gangsta Ock noticed one chick, who was eying him. She was bad, but he could tell she was a little tipsy.

The two talked for a while, getting to know each other, while his men and her friends went separate ways. They clung to each other quickly, as if they'd known each other for years.

They ended up leaving together and going to his place.

Hours later, the woman laid in his new crib, in his king size bed, naked after hours of rough, sweaty sex.

The sex was great for Gangsta Ock, the first piece of pussy since he'd been home. He started shooting blanks after his 3rd or 4th nut, but he was still working.

Gangsta Ock hadn't had a chance to actually think about the events that had recently taken place, since he walked out of that airport.

Shit was moving too fast and Gangsta Ock had dived nose first into action, which had resulted in murdering a Miami drug lord.

Gangsta Ock looked at the pretty female lying next to him, shaking his head. He'd promised himself that he would marry a woman before he laid the pipe in her. He wanted to follow his religion's marriage before sex rule, but that was out of the question now.

The pussy was amazing, but shawty had to go. He didn't feel right sleeping over with a bitch he'd just met. Gangsta Ock thought to himself as he woke her up.

"Ashley, wake up." He shook the beautiful chick's leg while she was in a deep sleep. "Ashely," he shook her a little harder.

She awoke, looking annoyed. As soon as her vision cleared, she smiled. "What is it?"

Gangsta Ock smelled her breath. "What the fuck, shawty? That can't be your breath smelling like ass," he stated with his face scrunched up. "I got some Colgate toothpaste in the bathroom," Gangsta Ock said, covering his mouth.

The young woman got up quickly and ran to the bathroom, feeling ashamed, embarrassed, and nasty.

As he got dressed, he made a note in his mind not to kiss her again, especially after all the nasty shit they'd done.

Once she came out of the bathroom in her booty shorts and bra, she walked up to him to give him a kiss, blushing because he laid that dick game down on her so good she went to sleep.

"I'll take a hug, sexy," he said, leaning in for the hug.

"Boy, stop playing. I just brushed my teeth. It was the liquor and seafood I ate," she said defiantly.

"I don't be doing the kissing shit anyway," he stated.

"Nigga, you just kissed me."

"That? Oh, that was a onetime thing."

"That's how it is after I sucked your dick and your stanky ass balls all night?" she said with an attitude, sitting on the edge of the bed with her arms crossed.

Gangsta Ock looked at her with a smirk that spoke volumes.

"Ashley, I know it wasn't your first, and maybe not your last time sucking dick. I'm very sure of that," Gangsta Ock stressed.

The sexy female felt disrespected. She slowly got up and began to get dressed. She couldn't believe her ears. As she was putting on her pants, she stopped and looked up at Gangsta Ock. He had her fucked up for another bitch.

"For your fucking information, you ugly ass Terry Crews, overbuilt ass nigga, my name ain't Ashley. It's Shea, you dumb motherfucker," she yelled.

Gangsta Ock just stood there looking crazy, really ready to choke her.

"I don't go around sucking everybody dick, or fucking niggas. I'm not a thot."

"I can't tell," he mumbled.

"What? I only let you fuck because I liked you and your vibe," Shea said while tears were now running down her face as she finished getting dressed.

Gangsta Ock looked at her as if she was crazy. His mind was still on some jail, in the yard shit, lifting weights with a knife on him, ready for war.

"Bitch! You need to get the fuck out my crib with all that shit," Gangsta reiterated as he passed her all of her belongings.

Shea knew she couldn't beat a man, she was only 5'5" in height. Tears stained face, which turned into a wicked grin. She reached in her purse and pulled out pepper spray. Then she sprayed Gangsta Ock, who didn't see it coming.

That wasn't it. She kicked him in his nuts as he screamed in pain.

"You crazy, bitch," he shouted as flashbacks of riots and fights played in his mind because the police always sprayed everyone with mace to stop the mayhem.

"You damn right I'm crazy, you disrespectful mother-fucka," Shea scoffed over him as he was literally on his knees.

Gangsta Ock headed to the bathroom, but ran into the wall, dropping to his knees as he rubbed his eyes, only making it worse. Once he made it inside his bathroom, he splashed water in his face, but he was still having a hard time getting it out. "What the fuck you do that for, shawty? I ain't put hands on you, slim," Gangsta Ock shouted, wiping his eyes with a washcloth, trying to get his vision back intact.

"Nigga, I'm not no man, but I won't let no fuck nigga disrespect me," she said in her country accent laced with a little Créole.

"I ain't mean to disrespect you."

"You lucky that's all I did," Shea stated, fully dressed, standing at his bathroom door, about to leave.

"You can lose my number," Shea said, leaving.

Gangsta Ock didn't mean a word he spoke to her. He was just being himself. He knew beautiful women like Shea were hard to pull, especially as ugly as he was.

Plus, her pussy and head game was top notch, he needed her. He now respected shawty's gangster as well. She wasn't taking no shit.

"Shea, I'm sorry. Please don't leave. I ain't mean that shit, shawty. It just be hard for me to trust people. The jails raised me, and sometimes I have a fucked-up way of thinking," he said.

She stopped and listened, while he was still cleaning his eyes. She turned around, facing him and looking him in his eyes. She couldn't help but feel for the somber expression that was plastered on his face.

"Shea, I'm sorry. I was being an ass. It won't happen again. I like you too. Well just a little bit now that I may not be able to have kids," he said, making her laugh.

She put her purse down, debating on if she should stay or not, while standing at the front door.

Look at the look on his face. He do look kinda good, and seems to have all the qualities a true man should possess, she thought to herself. *I should make his big ass beg some more, but his apology is more than enough.*

"Okay. Now come to the sink so I can get that shit out your eyes," she said with a laugh, grabbing Gangsta Ock's hand and leading him back to the sink.

Once his vision was restored. Gangsta Ock went into his huge kitchen and went to work on the stove, preparing breakfast.

Luckily, he'd gone shopping the previous day and Art had looked out for him, giving him a BMW truck, 200,000 dollars, and a crib.

Shea sat amazed by how Gangsta Ock maneuvered in a kitchen, like a true chef. She sat in his dining room, watching him work, with a towel over his shoulder.

"Damn, maybe I did just find my knight in shining armor, a man who cooks for a woman," she said.

"You damn right," he stated.

After preparing breakfast, they both ate, while stealing glimpses of each other. It was then Gangsta Ock noticed how radiant her honey colored skin was. Her walnut color eyes brought out her features even more.

"So tell me more about you, Shea."

Her ruby red pouty lips smiled before she spoke. "What is it you would like to know, Gangsta Ock?"

"How about you call me Justin, for starters, smart ass," he said, making her laugh.

"First name basis, my type. You must plan on having me around for a while," she stated.

"Not a while, Shea, but forever if you're the woman you portray you are."

"Believe me, I am who I say I am."

"Ok, Eminem, well I want to know for my own personal reasons, being that you're going to be around forever." His words caused her stomach to flutter. She couldn't stop smiling. It felt like a dream come true. "Well, I'm 23 years old and a college student, who attends Miami University. I'm majoring in criminal justice. I want to be a lawyer. I am a part time licensed nurse. I'm independent, single, no kids, and happy." She spoke with such confidence as she put a piece of pancake in her mouth.

Gangsta Ock laughed at her last remark. He admired everything about her. His New York niggas would say "ma is spicy, son."

"What's so funny? What the hell is funny?"

"Nothing, you just smart and beautiful."

"What do you do for a living?" Shea questioned, stuffing a fork full of eggs over easy in her mouth, hoping to get the last laugh.

"I'm a gay male stripper," he stated.

She almost choked on a piece of sausage. She knew it was too good to be true with him.

Gangsta Ock started dying laughing. The look on her face was as if she shitted herself.

"Naw, boo, I'm joking. I just came home from doing a 15-year bid in the feds, but I'm a licensed personal trainer," he informed her.

"Oh yeah? Good, I need to get toned."

"I don't do drugs, nor do I sell them, but I am a Gangsta, who lives a gangsta life, but I'm also on my clean Islam," Gangsta Ock spoke with a serious expression.

Shea knew he wasn't joking. That same look he possessed, her brother had, also. She was impressed by his honesty, but she knew a thug nigga wasn't what she wanted in life.

"Justin, my brother lives that same lifestyle, and you will only get out what you put in. The only outcome is jail or death, and I want neither one for you, being that we just met and I like you." She showcased her pretty smile.

"I like you, too, but you sound like my P.O." He said, smiling, seeing she cared.

"Boy, shut up."

"Seriously though. Where you get that new Benz coupe from, with a LN nurse job?" Gangsta smiled.

The two talked until daylight hit.

***

Jacksonville, FL

It was a quarter to twelve, and Lil Snoop was just coming back from checking on a couple of his traps in the projects he ran around the city.

Lil Snoop was born in Chicago but raised in Jacksonville and Carol City in Miami, which had been his residence for some years now.

Not to mention, he was the head of the Gangsta Disciples in Jacksonville, and he had over five hundred niggas under him.

Growing up on the south side of Chicago with two parents that were known gangbangers was rough on his childhood.

Lil Snoop got his name from his family, because he looked like Snoop Dogg. When he was six years old, he started boxing, kickboxing, and practicing martial arts, just to defend himself from other gangs.

For the last couple of years, he and his team of young killers had made a heavy name for themselves. Now, being down with a nigga like Savage, they were untouchable.

Lil Snoop pulled up to South Beach in an Audi A8, looking for Savage. His first cousin, Lil Shooter, was the only reason Savage had brought him into the family. It only helped that his name was ringing bells in the streets.

He saw Savage seated on the bench near the walkway, waiting for him. He was late.

Once he saw the youngin smiling with a bop in his walk, Savage shook his head. Lil Snoop took a seat next to him.

"I'm sorry about being late, boss. Traffic was heavy across the bridge," Lil Snoop stated, looking at all the bitches in bikinis walking the beach and tanning.

"Lateness is a sign of disrespect and laziness. Don't let it happen again," Savage said in a serious tone, staring in Lil Snoop's beady eyes.

"Now to cut straight to the point, that shit you pulled last night could've been deadly. Next time, stop and think, not only about yourself, but about the whole team," Savage said.

Lil Snoop just listened to him without saying a word.

"You're only 18, but you're smarter than most. Use your brains. Anybody can kill, but it's about how you kill, and when. I depend on you for a lot of shit, whether you know it or not. You a little brother to me and the gang. We just need you to be more on point."

Lil Snoop nodded his head, knowing it was real. "I will, I got you," he said smoothly.

"We about to have a lot of shit going on, so I need everyone to have their head in the game," Savage stated.

"I know, cuz."

"Hope so, because you may lose everything, including your life, if you're not focused," he stated seriously.

"That's life."

"Once the Zoe Pound find out we killed Sam, they going to come. And when I say come, I mean extra hard. Last night only triggered it. You're not new to the streets, or killing, but look at the big picture," he said staring into the sunny, bright clouds.

"You're right, I never took the time to see from a bird's eye view like this, big homie. So thank you," he stated.

"Of course, this is why I'm here," Savage replied.

"Oh, I forgot to tell you, it's a nigga named Super in my hood who just came out the wood works, but he ran with the MPM niggas," Lil Snoop revealed.

"I think I know him," Savage pondered, feeling himself get a hard on from the mentioning of MPM, because most of them were dead, in prison, or MIA.

"Ok. Snatch him up and have some fun until I come through. I want to holla at the boy before I kill him," Savage spoke nonchalantly as he stood to his feet.

"I got you, folk. That's on everything, cuz," Lil Snoop said as both men embraced each other and then went their separate ways to attend to their business.

Romell Tukes

Chapter 8

Downtown Miami

Savage arrived at the five-star restaurant on Collins Ave. to meet Jada for their lunch get-together.

He walked in, looking like a young boss in His Emporia Armani suit. He walked to his regular booth in the back, where he always sat when he came to this fancy restaurant.

The restaurant was full of rich white people on their lunch breaks, or just there on business.

Jada was sitting at the table waiting on him, looking sexy as hell in her tight, black Versace strapless dress, with a pair of red bottoms on her feet. She looked like an actress, straight out of Hollywood.

Once Savage reached the table, Jada stood and greeted him with a hug. They held one another for a few seconds.

"Damn," Savage said, inhaling the strong scent of her Chloe perfume and looking at her wide curvy hips that fit in perfectly with her flat stomach.

Savage couldn't help but eye every curve that could be seen through her dress, which exposed her thick smooth thighs.

"You looking real good, Jada. I'm glad to see you," Savage said, remembering the time she was doing bad, like a bum on the street, due to her crack habit.

"Same here, Mr. Savage," she said, smiling at him and looking him up and down.

"Nigga, please," he joked.

"Nah, for real, you looking real sexy in that business suit. You look like Steve Harvey," she said as they both laughed.

A pretty white woman approached their table with a notepad and pen. The waitress was a college student at FSU.

"Would you like to order now that your guest has arrived," the waitress asked in a low pitch voice, showing her white teeth.

"Yes, I'm hungry as hell. Can we both get the number nine and steak, well done, please," Savage said without even looking at the menu.

"Okay, and drinks?" she asked, writing everything down.

"Just two waters, please."

"Ok, on its way," she said, walking off and trying her best to switch her flat ass. Her ass was so small and flat that her back pockets touched each other.

"You must come here a lot," Jada said, looking around.

"On business," he replied.

After a couple of minutes of talking and catching up, their food arrived, and they began eating.

Jada looked a little nervous as she looked around to see if she recognized anybody, because this was Big Zoe's type of crowd also.

She wore extra makeup today, just for that reason. She also wore her hair in a bun, normally she would have it hanging down to her shoulders.

"Are you okay? You look nervous and scared, as if the boogieman is after you," Savage stated with a laugh, while eating.

"I see you're still a smart ass," Jada smiled

"Of course."

"It's good to see you doing good. You always had that drive, and passion for success. I sometimes feel as if you forgot about little ole me." Jada gave off a sad look.

"I could never forget about you. Shit, we was in the sandbox together, me, you, Britt, Big D, and Bama. Remember them days?" he said as she nodded, placing a fake smile on her face. The sound of Britt's name made her stomach turn. She had always been her rival.

"You'll always be a piece of my heart. We friends, Jada I will always be here for you. Never question that," Savage spoke sincerely.

Jada's panties became saturated with her juices, yet again, from the sound of his voice. Jada knew she had to fight her true feelings. She didn't want to put herself out there.

"How's life and business going for you?" She asked, trying to change the subject before she trapped herself.

"I'm rich, happy, and alive, thanks to Allah," Savage replied. "Oh, I forgot to tell you Bama, well Abdulla, as he likes to be called now, won his appeal."

"Naw, you joking," she said, shocked.

"His lawyer got at me, so I'm happy. And I'm happy he's coming home to fall back into life. Everything is too good right now," Savage informed her.

"That's great, Savage. I just hope he truly changed, because it's a little different out here now," Jada stated, sipping on her glass of water.

"Facts," he replied.

"I also heard your crew tore down Big Zoe's club. What was that all about, bad boy?" she questioned.

"It was a little misunderstanding. You know how niggas do with a little bit of liquor in their system."

"Yeah, I guess," she said, shrugging her shoulders.

"So how are the two of y'all doing? You two look so happy together," he asked, fishing.

"I'm sure you know looks can be deceiving, but he is a good man. He's a little jealous of you, but I told him," she said.

"Told him what?" he asked.

"We just family. What else would I tell him? That nigga crazy. He gotta respect our friendship," she said, being honest.

"I can dig it," he replied.

"Yeah, lately he been so busy trying to find who killed his friend, Sam. that shit was all over the news. I met him before. He was cool, but that fucked him up."

"Damn. He was a good nigga," Savage replied, giving off a sad look.

"Oh, now that you mention it, I overheard him say his team of security got a witness, so hopefully soon he'll find out who did that crazy shit," Jada spoke freely, eating her steak while pushing the gravy to the side because she hated gravy.

Savage's mind went from zero to sixty, so he thought it would be best to change the subject. He didn't want to alert her. He didn't know where her loyalty lied.

"How's your child? You got a son, right? I saw him on your page?" He said.

"He's good, but bad as hell. OMG, this little nigga is a handful, but I love being a mommy. It feels so good," Jada said.

"We should set up a play date with them, if you down?" He asked.

"Hell yeah, I'm always free for that. I spend most of my time babysitting anyway," Jada took him up on his offer.

"What do you have planned for the future, Jada, now that you married with a child? I can't see you being the housewife type forever," Savage said, finishing his meal.

"To be honest, I'm just focused on a couple internet businesses, happiness, and raising my son to be a better man than his father. Not saying his father isn't a good man, because he is a good father and provider, but his lifestyle isn't what I plan to be a part of forever," she said, being honest.

She really wanted to tell him that she wanted him in her future, and not Big Zoe's little dick ass, but thought better of it.

How about you, black Bill Gates, or Jay-Z, young Hov," she said, mocking him, knowing Jay-Z was his favorite rapper besides DMX.

"I just want to remain alive so I can enjoy what I worked so hard to stay alive and out of jail for. Plus, seeing Lil Smoke grow up is my best achievement in life. I'm just thankful, Jada, I can't lie," Savage said, thinking about his little brother.

After the two talked for another hour, they knew it was time to go.

"It's about time for me to get going," she said as her phone kept vibrating.

"Me too," he said, checking the time on his Bust Down watch.

"I'll be hitting you up for that playdate with the kids," Savage said, getting up.

"Ok," she said gathering her purse.

"You look stunning, Jada. Thank you for your time, "Savage said, hugging her.

"Sure," she said, feeling so weak and lonely in his arms that she didn't want to let him go, but she had to.

The two departed with their own thoughts in their heads. One was full of lust, and the other was trying to figure out who could be the witness that saw Sam's murder.

***

Sam's funeral was a closed casket funeral because his killer shot his face off, leaving it very hard to identify him. Thank god for his teeth and dental records, which made it easy to identify the burnt man.

Burning down the house was a brilliant idea, leaving him looking like a disfigured monster from a scary movie.

The funeral was held in a church in North Miami. The funeral home couldn't have given him a face lift, even if they had Dr. Miami working on him.

Sam's funeral was packed, as if it was a club on a Friday night. The funeral was over three hours long, with all types of people in the church, FBI agents, kingpins, his friends, family, enemies, and powerful people.

The whole city came out to be a part of this funeral, even people who didn't know the powerful man.

Blocks were shut down until after the funeral service, it was so real.

After Pastor Tyrell Carver gave his long speech, people gave their farewell speeches, while Big Zoe sat in the front row with a ten man security team, wondering who would want to do something so gruesome to a good man.

Sam never crossed him nor did him any type of way to make him see a fucked up side to him. What would make someone want to kill him? Sam was strictly a businessman, no matter if you were poor or rich.

Big Zoe was like a son to him, so he was going to make it his business to find his killer using witnesses, police reports, and whatever else it would take to repay his beloved mentor.

There was one thing heavy on his mind, and that was why Savage wasn't present. That wasn't sitting well with Zoe.

Why wouldn't he pay his respects to the man who made him successful? It didn't make sense to him.

After the funeral, Big Zoe stayed for a few minutes to pay his last respects to his friend alone.

He was distracted by a beautiful woman crying next to Sam's grave, with a young man standing next to her.

She wore a nice Valentino slit dress, with six inch heels and a black, small mink coat. The lady looked white, or mixed with something exotic.

The man wore a black Gucci suit. He was light skinned and handsome, as if he had good genes.

Big Zoe wondered who they were, so he took it upon himself to approach them. There was just something that stood out about them.

"I'm sorry to interrupt the two of you, but is everything okay?" Big Zoe questioned knowing it wasn't as he looked at her puffy blue eyes.

The woman nodded her head as he looked at Big Zoe, wondering where he came from and why he was so black and ugly.

"Yeah, we good, fam, but thank you," the young man said, consoling the woman, who was wiping her tears and getting herself together.

"If y'all don't mind me asking, how do y'all know Sam? I'm pretty sure you two not from around here," Big Zoe said.

"We're from New York, the Bronx, and Sam is my mother's ex-husband, and my father," the young man stated, surely catching Zoe off guard to see the awkward look on his face.

Big Zoe remembered him speaking of an ex-wife, but never a child. As far as he knew, he didn't have any kids.

Big Zoe was seriously in awe because he didn't expect for him to say that. He wondered why he'd never seen them before. "Is it a lie, scam, or act?" he thought.

The man looked just like Sam, but with a creamy complexion and green eyes. He had his physique, nose, cheek bones, eyebrows, and swag. There was no denying it.

"Wow... I'm so sorry about your loss. I'm a very good friend of Sam. My name is Big Zoe. He was like a father to me. He raised me in the game," Big Zoe said.

He shook both of their hands. When the woman stood up, she had a crazy body, long blonde hair, medium height, sexy, flawless, nice lips, nice teeth, and she was all natural.

"No doubt, we appreciate that kind gesture, my guy," the young man said.

Big Zoe saw all kind of tattoos all over his body, red five point stars all over his neck, and shit with New York sports teams all over his arms.

"I can promise you both that I will find his killer, and deal with him," Big Zoe informed them.

"Thank you," the woman replied in a sweet low voice. It was her first time speaking. She was white, and mixed with Puerto Rican. She looked like a white girl, but she spoke Spanish.

Big Zoe had a couple questions for the young man.

"What's your name, youngin?" Big Zoe asked, trying not to stare at Sam's ex-wife too hard, but she was bad.

"My family call me Lil Sam, but my homies up north call me Stone," he informed Big Zoe, brushing his curly hair with his hand. He was tired and ready to get back up top.

"Okay, that's what's up, youngin. I'm glad you came to pay your respects. My parents died years ago, and I never made it to their funerals, and till this day it, still kills me," Big Zoe said as they listened.

"I feel you, son, that's a fact," Stone said, peeping the man's style. He was obviously somebody important, judging from his Salvatore Ferragamo suit and shoes to match.

"You're in a gang?" Big Zoe asked.

"Yeah, I'm the big homie for the P. Stone Bloods in New York. We doing big things up top. I'm sure you heard," Stone stated surely, as if he had.

"I believe I did hear about them, and the Empire niggas," Big Zoe said.

"Okay, yeah, those the Brim niggas. They official out there, fam," Stone replied.

"You seem like a somebody out here, especially dealing with a man like my father. My mother told me all the stories. Plus, who need ten linebackers with them at all times" Stone said laughing, looking outside to see Zoe's security team lined up.

Big Zoe laughed. "I run the Miami Zoe Pound out here. I own this city, thanks to your father. He played a big part in my career. Take my number, maybe we can link up. Text me ASAP so I can log you in.

Stone had heard all about the vicious Zoe Pound killers and drug traffickers. They were on gangland TV, the First 48, and the World News at least once a month.

"Ight, I got you," Stone said, texting his number real quick.

"I got a lot of shit going on. If you want to network, legal or illegal, but I may have a lead on your father's killer. If I call you, just know what's up," Big Zoe said.

"Say no more, I'll be waiting. I'ma fly my mom back up top. It was definitely a pleasure meeting you, homie. Hope to hear from you very soon." Stone shook Big Zoe's hand before walking off.

Romell Tukes

Chapter 9

Downtown Miami

Lil Sam, aka Stone, stared out of his balcony suite in the 5-star hotel, in downtown Miami. He was wearing an all red Balmain sweat suit.

He couldn't help but wonder why when shit started to go good in his life, it always took a turn for the worse.

Lil Sam received his street name from his best friend, Rosco, who was murdered years ago after a middle school fight. They both jumped the kid in front of his girl and beat him up over an argument in science class.

The kid had a gun in his backpack, which he didn't hesitate to use while getting jumped. Once he started shooting, everybody ran, except for Stone and Rosco. They were both shot. Rosco got shot in the heart twice, and Stone once in the leg.

Rosco died, which had a big effect on Stone. Years down the line, Stone ended up killing the kid who killed Rosco outside of a club. Lil Sam ran with the name out of respect for him. Stone was born in Yonkers, NY, which was located next to the Bronx.

Big Sam moved him and his mom there, once he was born, for a better life. Plus, the area was low key. Around that time, Sam was wanted for questioning in Tone's murder by the NYPD and homicide detectives.

Stone's father and mother got married while she was pregnant with him, Becky gave birth to Lil Sam at St. Joseph Hospital in Yonkers, NY.

Becky had been with Sam since middle school. She was always his ride or die, even when he did a state bid and met Tone, Savage's father, the one who Sam killed for killing his brother.

Becky was a beautiful woman. She looked like Olivia Culpo, but thicker, because she had a body of a southern black woman. She was Puerto Rican and white.

She had been loyal to Sam ever since day one, and while he climbed his way up the drug chain and became one of the biggest heroin dealers on the east coast.

Things were good in their life and marriage, but as time went by, Sam's infidelity caused mayhem within his marriage. Sam was cheating, lying, and even had women calling the crib as if it was nothing. Becky couldn't take it no more.

They finally got divorced and chose to co-parent with Lil Sam. Months later, the FBI picked up Sam at a gas station, after watching him for a few weeks.

The feds questioned him in an interrogation room about Tone's murder, and his number being the last in his call log.

Once the feds realized Sam was of no help and they had nothing on him, they had to let him go because they had no evidence to hold him in custody.

After that interaction, Sam thought it would be good to move and leave his family, just so his lifestyle wouldn't affect them in any way.

Sam's Cuban connect was in Miami, so they both thought it would be a good idea to relocate and network in other cities.

Without waiting to be snatched by the feds, Sam left New York. Becky was upset, having to raise a child on her own, but she knew once the feds were onto you, or wanted you, then they would do anything to get you.

Sam left Becky and his son a huge mansion in Long Island, a condo in Manhattan, three luxury cars, over two million dollars, and some properties, just in case she ran out of money.

He also sent her money through Western Union every month to make sure his family was good while he was taking over Miami.

As time went on, Becky found herself a rich white doctor, who was a good man and really loved her. The two moved in together in a penthouse in Manhattan and enjoyed life while raising Lil Sam.

Unlike most kids, Lil Sam didn't follow other kids. With the blood of a hustler, Lil Sam grew up too fast and decided to pave his own way in life after he graduated from High School.

After graduation, his father sent him a BMW coupe, hoping he would attended college and continue his education. He was very smart, with an IQ of 140.

Stone had different plans for his life, and college wasn't it. He was already gangbanging and in the streets with his gang.

Once he found a Dominican connect in Washington Heights, it was over. He started moving bricks. Then he saw his future.

Having a big influence on teenagers and adults in his hood in the Bronx and all over New York, he was able to gain a big army of goons from every borough.

As time passed, he'd become a big homie for his blood set, P. Stone Bloods. They'd become the most cold hearted organization since Pistol Pete and the SMM crew out of the Sound View section in the Bronx.

Stone stared up into the sky blue clouds, hoping Big Zoe found his father's killer, because they were close. Even though he was distant in miles, Sam was still a good father. He knew Big Zoe would make it happen. It was only a matter of time.

Stone understood this could be a new beginning with Big Zoe. Maybe he could open up shop in Miami. It would be nothing to send a crew down there and build his own little empire down south.

He looked at his Rolex, realizing it was still early. His mom was in her room sleep, and their flight left a little later in the evening. He had plans to take his mom out for lunch, to the beach, and shopping, because he knew that would lighten her up a little.

***

Britt was up early, getting herself together to spend time with her family, since she didn't have school today, just some studying later.

There were light footsteps running towards the kitchen, where she was cooking breakfast with Ms. Jackson. She already knew who it was.

"Stop running," Britt shouted before she even saw Lil Smoke.

"Sorry," Lil Smoke said in his soft kid voice as he tiptoed into the kitchen in his Hulk pajamas, ready to start his day.

"Thank you," Britt said, looking at his fuzzy braids.

"Good morning, big sis and nanny, me hungry," he said, pulling out a chair from under the table.

"Good morning, baby. Big sis is fixing you some pancakes and fried eggs," Britt said, flipping pancakes on the stove.

Ms. Jackson squeezed fresh orange juice for them all, as she did every morning, instead of buying Sunny D orange juice.

"I got a full day set up today, so make sure you eat up. You're going to need it," Britt said, placing a plate in front of Lil Smoke as he began to eat it.

"Y'all spoil that boy," Ms. Jackson stated, sitting down.

"Yeah, that's all Savage's work. But are you hungry, Ms. Jackson?" asked Britt.

"No, child, I ate already, with Savage, before he left this morning. I made a plate for the both of you, too. It's in the oven, but I see you was eager to cook," Ms. Jackson said, smiling as Britt frowned, and then smiled.

"Sis, where is my brother?" Lil Smoke asked with his mouth full.

"Boy, don't talk with food in your mouth. I tell you about that all the time," Ms. Jackson said.

"Ok," he said, not trying to get slapped in his head.

Britt hated when he asked that because she felt as if Savage should be there with him more. She made a mental note to check him on that ASAP, before Lil Smoke started feeling abandoned.

As soon as she was about to answer, Savage walked into the kitchen carrying four big bags.

Savage was wearing a Givenchy suit with his dreads hanging down his back and out of breath. Lil Smoke hopped off his chair with one leap and ran to his brother, almost knocking his food over trying to see what was in the bags.

"What's in the bag?" Lil Smoke asked with a wicked smile.

Savage laughed hard as his little brother pressed him for the bags. He pulled out a big box with an Iron Man toy inside.

"Oh snap," he said, snatching the toy and running upstairs, leaving his food on the table. He ran to his room without saying thank you.

Britt yelled for him to come back and finish his breakfast, but it was useless.

"Thanks honey," she said with an attitude, cleaning off the table.

"Don't be a party crusher, boo, but what happened to school?" he asked, sitting down.

"If you listen, I told you I ain't have class today," she said, placing a dish in the sink, and then wiping down Lil Smoke's mess.

"I got something for you, too," Savage said, pulling out a box from a Tiffany and Company bag.

Britt's weight shifted to her left leg as her right hand went to her hip. She was ready to tell Savage about himself, until he popped open the box.

There was a diamond neckless sitting perfectly in the box it was shining.

"Ohh. Thank you, baby." Britt kissed him while he grabbed a hand full of her ass in her Yves Saint Laurent booty shorts.

"Excuse us, Ms. Jackson, but we're going upstairs," Britt said, getting wet.

"Ok, please go," she replied laughing.

"Can you watch Lil Smoke and have him dressed and ready in an hour so we can go to the amusement park, please?" Britt asked.

"Yes. Now go get y'all freak on," Ms. Jackson said laughing. She knew how the two got down because sometimes she would hear the moans through the thick walls.

Savage and Britt ran upstairs faster than Lil Smoke had minutes prior. They made love for an hour all over their bedroom. Britt came four times to his two times, but it was the best quickie ever.

***

Big Sandy USP

Abdulla was walking on the prison yard track, enjoying the hot summer heat in his gray shorts and gray shirt to match his gray New Balances, which were sold on commissary for $80.

It was his normal routine every morning with his celly, Mice, who was Britt's older brother.

His morning routine was to wake up when the doors pooped open at 6am, eat some oatmeal, pray, email friends and family, go to the yard to exercise for an hour or an hour and a half. He would work out with his celly, and then walk the yard.

"Ahkee, my future is becoming bright, as far as freedom. Allah is giving me a second chance at life," Abdulla said.

"I feel you, Bama, but don't take it for granted, please. I saw so many niggas come back and forth, bruh," Mice said. He was the only one who still called him Bama.

"You right. My drive is too crazy to come back, bro. I was a kid when I came in. I was a drug dealer, murderer, and robber, but now I'm a Muslim, who wants better for all of my brothers. I just hope I can get Savage to see it that way," Abdulla said with a serous expression.

"I'ma be honest, people ain't living right out there, bro. The world is the devil's playground for the disbelievers," Mice stated.

"Paradise is for the believers," Abdulla said, finishing his sentence.

"Stay awake and focus on your own mission." Mice started walking away from some inmates talking about getting a nigga out the spot because he stole someone radio.

"I fear if I go back, I may lose sight of what path Allah chose for me to walk down," Abdulla said sadly.

"You found yourself. Most people die not being able to do that. Go out there and stand for something, or you will fall for anything," Mice said, giving encouraging words.

"You right."

"I'm never coming home. I have no more appeals. I'ma die in a USP, like most of us will. Shit, I'ma die in a outside hospital, if I'm blessed. I want you to understand that Allah chose you. He saw something in you, so don't let him down," Mice spoke like a true friend as they walked past a group of MS-13 Mexicans doing mandatory workouts, all burpees.

They walked the rest of the yard for twenty minutes, chopping it up before he went back to court. Before the move ended, everybody was on the ground as the tower guard dropped a loud conscious bomb, trying to stop the fight on the hand ball court.

A Mexican was getting stabbed up by two Mexicans. It was a hit from one of their big homies.

The Mexicans didn't stop stabbing the man until a live round from a shotgun was shot in the air.

By the time the guards and the first and second team response come out, the Mexican was dead, not moving, with no pulse. And they still tried to strap the dead man to the stretcher.

The nurses didn't even try to bring him back to life. He was just another dead young man who died on their yard with only 16 days left before he went home to his family.

Chapter 10

Zoe Fresh was sitting behind the wheel of an all-black crown Victoria with dark tints, the kind the detectives drive in the hood.

He was leaned back in his seat, watching the mosque on North Blvd, and everyone coming in and out.

It was Jommah Friday, so it was packed with Muslim women, who were fully covered, as well as kids and men. He'd been parked there for six hours, but it was well worth it because his targets were inside praying.

Zoe Fresh had no clue that the two niggas he was looking for were Muslim. Their well-groomed dreads should have been a dead giveaway, but he overlooked it.

Minutes later, he saw Gangsta Ock and Big Art walk out, both in white garments that he would've loved to turned red. Zoe Fresh massaged the 50 Cal gun in his lap, as if it was a cat, when he saw Savage walk out with a beautiful light skin female by his side. He couldn't wait for the greenlight.

His boss just wanted him to do some research on the crew before making his decision because he needed to be sure his instinct was correct.

Big Art and Gangsta Ock hopped in a Yukon truck with rims and tints, and pulled out of the parking lot.

Gangsta Ock saw a black Crown Vic parked up the block, but he wasn't sure if someone was in there. It just looked out of place to him.

"Ahkee, the Iman is leaving to move back to New York soon. I believe his wife is ill, so he told us he wouldn't be coming back. We gotta holla at Savage so he can replace him soon," Big Art said, stopping at a red light and looking at all of the luxury cars speeding on the opposite side of the street.

"We should've just hollered at him, Ock. We need a good Iman, bruh, I was getting sick of these jail Imams," Gangsta Ock said, shaking his head.

"Naw, him and Britt going out to eat."

"She Muslim? I didn't even see her sitting in the back," Gangsta Ock asked, wondering. There was a no denying it, Britt was a bad bitch. She reminded him of a light skinned Stacy Dash, from back in the day.

"No. I don't think so, cuz," Art stated, looking at the Miami citizens roll up and down the streets in skates.

"I just got me a new little chick."

"Oh yeah, slim. But how old? Let me find out you jump trees," Art said, laughing, being the comedian he was sometimes.

"Nah, she in her twenties. I like her, ahkee. She a real bitch and she be taken my mind off shit," he said.

"What's her name, Bruce Jenner?" Big Art said, cracking up at his own jokes.

"Yoooo, slim, you on some bullshit right now," Gangsta Ock said with a chuckle. "Her name Shea," he continued with a large smile, thinking about her fire pussy.

"Damn, nigga, you fresh home, and already cuffing these hoes? You tender dick nigga," Big Art said, driving down Collins Ave on his way to South Miami to pick up some money from Liberty City.

"I'm serious, bruh, I like shawty," Gangsta Ock smiled.

"I'm happy for you, but don't let her get you off track. Most of these hoes is sack chasing. Pussy is a real live lethal weapon I seen that shit take a lot of good men out," big Art said.

"Facts, bruh bruh."

"We got a meeting later at the barbershop, so I'ma drop you off. Meet me over there. I gotta go to Liberty City real quick," he said, pulling over at Gangsta Ock's apartment.

***

University of Miami

Shea couldn't focus at school at all. She was barely able to take notes, she was so mind fucked.

Her thoughts were on one person only, and that was Gangsta Ock. They'd been spending a lot of time together, and she loved every second of it. There was no doubt about it.

She couldn't help but smile at how many times she made his big muscle head ass almost cry from her amazing blow jobs. It would make any nigga cry, she had a talent.

She walked out the science building towards the parking lot where her pearl white Benz was parked every day.

Once her phone started to ring, she rushed to get her iPhone out of her Burberry purse, hoping it was her boo.

Looking at her caller ID, her entire mood changed. Once she saw who the caller was, she did not want to pick up, so she hesitated.

"Omg. What do you want?" she answered her phone without giving the caller a chance to say hi to her.

"Slow the fuck down. Who do you think you're talking to, Shea? You better learn to respect me. Let's make this your last time," the male caller stated.

"Whatever, nigga."

"First off, don't call me by my government on the phone, Shea. Now where were you this weekend?" Zoe Fresh asked his little sister.

"Nigga, last time I checked, I was grown, and my parents were dead," she said with a big attitude, mad at him for trying to ruin her life from behind the scene.

"Stop being so hard-headed and answer."

"Why are you trying to question me?" she replied, getting inside her car. It was so hot out that she had sweat drops on her forehead. She wore a Hermes sundress and sunglasses.

"Shea, I'm not one of your friends at school, or who you party with. I'm your brother, who fucking raised you," he informed her with a serious tone.

"I know, Zoe Fresh. I don't have time to argue. I'm driving. Can you text me?" she asked sarcastically.

"No, I don't text, but why you didn't visit our parents' gravesites?" He really wanted to know.

"I didn't feel like it, Zoe. I don't move when you say move. I have to go," she said, hanging up in his face while driving.

She hated going to her parents' gravesite. It always got her in a depressed phase that was hard to snap back from. Right now, she was in a good space, mentally and emotionally, but he wouldn't understand or care. She still loved him because she knew his intentions were good.

***

Zoe Fresh stood at his parents' gravesite, thinking about the conversation he had with his sister.

He knew she hated going to their parents' gravesite, and he never pressured her, he only asked.

When their parents died of cancer, he was left to raise his baby sister, with the help of their grandmom.

It wasn't easy raising a little sister with a disabled grandmom, but he did, and he did it well.

He'd turned to the streets for money. He was never a drug dealer. He was a known hitman and robber. But if he robbed someone, then they were as good as dead.

After years of killing, he became one of the most dangerous Haitians in the state, and a paid hitman.

Shea knew her brother lived a dangerous lifestyle, but it got her into college, a Benz, and a two-bedroom apartment.

He just wanted what was best for her, so he was strict with her all the time.

***

Big Zoe pulled up at a nice mini-mansion near Sam's burned down house. He was with four of his goons, all dressed in suits, just like him.

"Big Moe, wait in the car for us. Keep it running. Is that too hard for your fat ass?" Big Zoe asked him before climbing out of the Lincoln truck.

"No, I'll be here, sir," Big Moe replied

"Iight, sucker," Big Zoe chuckled as he walked with three of his goons to the door.

Big Moe felt like he was a bitch. But when Big Zoe was long gone, he started popping shit.

Big Moe was a big boy, and he wasn't a bitch. He had a mean body count, and Big Zoe knew this. They both went to high school together, and had been friends ever since. But now he was a changed made nigga.

Big Moe had plans on being the man, soon. Unbeknownst to Big Zoe, he was about to make an attempt on Savage and his crew's lives, hoping to start a war, all because he got knocked out.

If Big Zoe found out, he'd be a dead man. But he didn't care anymore.

***

Big Zoe rang the doorbell, and he and his crew waited for the door to be answered.

From behind the door, an old white woman looked through her small peephole. She thought they were salesmen dressed in business suits, or Jehovah's Witnesses.

The older lady opened the door with a smile, showing her yellow teeth.

"Hey, who are-" Before she could say another word, Big Zoe's goons kicked her door in, knocking her to the floor.

Big Zoe and his crew rushed into her home with guns drawn, looking for anything alive and moving.

"Please, don't hurt me. I'm here by myself. My husband's at work." The old lady spoke through her crystal clear blue eyes.

She looked to be in her early 60's, but a person could tell 30-20 years ago she was a very beautiful woman. Her hair had a few strands of grey, but she had decent breasts, and wrinkles on her face.

She was confused as to why these black men were in her home. This was her reason for hating black people, and the reason she'd taught her kids to hate them also.

"Please, tell me what you want," she insisted, looking up at them.

"Well, Ms. Steward, you failed to report that you saw the murder of your neighbor. So I'm here to hear the whole story. If I believe you, then I'll let you live, old bitch," Big Zoe snarled.

"My husband is the chief of police. You won't make it down the road, you nigger," the old lady retorted.

Big Zoe laughed. Then he started pistol whipping her so hard it echoed through the house.

"You going to talk now?"

"No," she said, leaking blood.

"Ok. Trav and Mookie, do y'all thing," Big Zoe said as they both got undressed, ass naked.

The old lady saw their big dicks and prayed that they wasn't about to do what she was thinking.

They started raping her, one in her pussy, and one in her ass.

"Ohhh, uggghhh, nooo. Stop, ugghh," she screamed as two big dicks tore her walls apart.

"Uggh, shitt, yesss," she moaned, starting to like being raped. She started fucking back. Her titties bounced up and down. Big Zoe was shocked at the old lady. She was fucking like a porn star.

After both men came, she grabbed their dicks and sucked them clean with a crazy look on her face. It was her dream to get raped by two black guys with big dicks.

"Can you speak now? The next torment won't be so pleasurable," he said, still shocked by what he saw. The bitch was a straight freak.

"I saw three niggers standing outside while five blacks went in and came out after all the shooting and loud noises. They had bags with them, and were all dressed in black. They all had masks on at first, but when they came out, most of them didn't." She spoke freely, feeling cum dripping down her hairy, bushy pussy, which was still good at 60 something.

"How tall?" Big Zoe asked.

"I don't remember. But they all had dreads, except them bald head two," she stated.

"Bitch, what else? You better speak," he spoke through clenched teeth with fire in his eyes.

"Their size," she started talking, but forgot what she was saying. She was still shaking from her climax, since she hadn't had one in twenty years.

"All over 6 feet, I believe," she said fast, wondering if the two black guys could fuck her again. The two guards wanted a piece of her again, also. Her pussy and ass was warm and wet.

Boom. Boom. Boom... Big Zoe shot her in the head. He already knew he was correct. It was Savage.

"Damn, I wanted to fuck her again, boss. Her shit was fire just like my old lady at home," one of his goons said as they exited the house. Big Zoe just so happen to see a picture of her and her husband, who was in a police uniform. Big Zoe recognized the face. It was the Chief of Police. He shook his head, knowing the police was about to turn the city up.

Chapter 11

Lil Shooter was in Jacksonville, on the north side, in Dirty Red's projects, talking to him and Lil Snoop about the next re-up and tonight's meeting.

Dirty Red and Lil Snoop were both young, feared, and respected. They ran every dangerous project and block in Jacksonville.

"Tell Savage we got that MPM nigga tied up across town. We caught him slipping last night, Blood." Dirty Red informed Lil Shooter, with two red flags hanging from his back pockets, representing his Brim blood set.

"Okay. We'll tell him tonight," Lil Shooter replied as he got down to business. "How many bricks you have left?" He asked Lil Snoop.

"I believe four, but it's about to be gone once my man BloodRaw come through," Lil Snoop stated proudly.

I'll have the Liberty City Boss drop them bricks off to you tonight after our meeting, and don't be late, Lil Snoop. And don't come a hunnid deep to the barbershop," Lil Shooter said, walking over to his Lexus truck. Two cars full of young goons were parked behind him.

"Let's head to Miami now so we can be early," Dirty Red stated as he walked over to his glossy red Donk that sat on 32" rims.

"Yeah, you right. You strapped, folk?" Lil Snoop asked, while Dirty Red laughed as if it was a joke. He lifted his shirt, revealing the handles of two 357's. "They're like a license," he smiled, revealing a mouth full of gold teeth.

Lil Snoop nodded and hopped in his all red '96 Impala. He pulled off, blasting Plies' song "100 years," leaving out of the projects behind Dirty Red.

The hood was out. The hustlers were hustling their work, gambling, and keeping their eyes open for jack-boys.

Most of the towns were on their team, except the Cubans and Mexican gangbangers. Jacksonville was mostly blood or kinfolk, thanks to Lil Snoop and Dirty Red.

***

Savage went to prepare for his second meeting today with his team. He'd just left his meeting with JoJo, discussing a new connect and better prices.

Savage set up the meeting in the back of his barbershop. Since he had an hour or so left, he sat down to watch the news while relaxing in his Lay-Z-Boy.

"Just in… This is Roxy Lee reporting live in the suburban part of Miami, where a horrific murder was discovered early today. Police are still on the scene, canvassing the area."

Savage thought he was seeing shit when he saw Sam's burnt down house in the background, but he wasn't. He grabbed his controller, turning up the volume to listen to every word.

"In back of me sits the home of Police Chief Frank Steward, whose wife MaryBeth Steward was found beaten badly and shot multiple times in her chest. It is unknown as to why this tragedy took place, but Miami Police aren't wasting any time investigating."

Savage's eyes were glued to the reporter as she went on.

"This is Roxy Lee reporting live from Miami News, back to Stacey."

Savage turned off the TV and tried to put two and two together. A few minutes passed before it dawned on him that Jada told him about a witness. It was Big Zoe. He was sending a message.

An hour later, his crew walked in, all on time, and took their assigned seats at the round table.

"It's good to see everybody on time for once. Am I being overthrown?" The whole room erupted in laughter. "Listen, I'm going to get right to business. We have a new connect. The work is just as good as, if not better than, our last connect, but at a lower price, so we should be on board with the Colombians next week," Savage spoke proudly. "We have Jacksonville on lock, thanks to Dirty Red and Lil Snoop. Miami will always be ours, thanks to us all," Savage said with a smile as he continued. "Also, we now have a serious problem with Zoe Pound."

Everyone sat straight up with their eyes glued to Savage.

"So he declaring war over the club incident?" Lil Snoop questioned.

"No. Zoe Pound killed the witness. I blame nobody but myself because there shouldn't even have been a witness," Savage said, sounding disappointed.

"How do you know it was our witness and the Zoe Pound did it?" Gangsta Ock questioned.

"That night at the club, Big Zoe told me there was a witness. I assume, well there's no assuming. I know she told them whatever she knew before they killed her, so the art of war is to strike first and kill the head so the body will fall," Savage stated. "Everybody stay strapped and be on point. The Zoe Pound is dangerous and sneaky." Savage stared every one of his men in their eyes. "They're probably on to us, so everybody stay with a team of savages at all times," Savage instructed them. "It's war time and we're all ready, gentlemen. This meeting is over until the next one," Savage said as he stood to leave.

Everybody made their way outside, talking about the new prices and how they should hit up the "KOD" tonight, just for the fuck of it. Once outside, everybody was about to head to their cars to prepare for a night out until a black Ford Taurus creeped up.

Savage was the only one who saw the car creeping with the lights off and the windows down. Savage reacted quickly, pulling out his P89 Ruger and starting to fire at the car.

There were bullets from high powered weapons coming out of each window. Gangsta Ock and Big Art took cover because both men were careless and left their weapons in the car.

Lil Shooter and the two youngins were bussing back as if they were in a double "O" seven movie. There were two men on feet, running and shooting from behind cars.

Savage couldn't get a good shot. Dirty Red shot two of the gunmen that were in the backseat of the moving car, while Lil Snoop tried to take out the driver, who he recognized from the club.

Savage took one of the gunmen down that was on foot with a headshot, while the other man zig-zagged, seeing an open shot at Dirty Red, whose back was turned. He was trying to make sure Lil Snoop was good.

Before Dirty Red had a chance to turn around, two hollow tips caught him in his back, causing him to fall face first.

Lil Snoop and Lil Shooter caught his killer as he tried to make a run for it. They gunned him down until both men ran out of bullets.

It was a nasty sight. Savage heard sirens from a distance, so he ran past his barbershop to his parking spot, and hopped in his car, with his team behind him.

Dirty Red was left on the curb, dead. They didn't want to leave him, but they'd done what was best, killed the man who killed him.

***

Big Moe sat in the passenger seat of the Ford Taurus with his little cousin driving towards a lake with two bodies in the back. The car was riddled with bullet holes and shattered windows.

"Moe, what if they know it was us?" Crazy Ra asked with nervousness in his tone. "I'm not trying to die, them nigga's is heavy out here in these streets," Crazy Ra spat.

"Listen, you little bitch! Keep your mouth shut, and you have nothing to worry about. Now pull over at the dead end so we can drop these bodies off." Big Moe's facial expression matched his tone.

***

The detectives were all over the middle of the street and in front of Savage's shop with caution tape securing the crime scene area.

The two detectives who were called to the scene were grimy, dirty cops, who worked for Big Zoe.

Once the detectives got the ID's off the dead bodies, they already knew that the dead were Big Moe's flunkies.

Detective Clayton looked at his partner, pulling out his phone to call Big Zoe.

Chapter 12

Big Zoe was sitting in his office at one of his clubs, watching a thick white stripper named Snow White go to work on the pole downstairs on the dance stage.

Big Zoe started pacing his office in anger because of the call he'd just received from his paid detectives.

"Why the fuck would this fat piece of shit make a move on his own behalf?" J-Bo asked Big Zoe.

"When was the last time you spoke to that fat son of a bitch?" Big Zoe asked J-Bo.

"The other day, boss. And now that I think about it, he was acting a little funny."

What you mean acting funny?" Big Zoe showed a disgruntled expression.

"He wasn't himself," J-Bo replied while smoking a swisher sweet filled with haze.

Big Zoe was in deep thought as he took a seat behind his desk trying to put two and two together as to why his longtime friend, who he'd known over 20 years, would snake him.

He thought back to the phone call from Det. Clayton.

"Your buddy, Big Moe, and his flunkies were involved in a shooting in front of a very well-known killer and drug dealer named Savage's barbershop."

Big Zoe shook off the phone call with plans for Big Moe, if he was to arrive any time soon.

Big Zoe hated snitches and snakes, and Big Moe was going to be made an example.

***

Savage and Big Art sat in the prayer room of Savage's mansion, wondering how them nigga's got the drop on them so soon.

"I really underestimated them, Big Art," Savage stated, shaking his head. "The hit was sloppy. You never supposed to let your enemy see you coming. That's why I think this wasn't from Big Zoe," informed Savage.

"I feel the same way. Lil Snoop said one of them niggas he beat up at the club that night was the driver," Big Art said while cleaning off his tray pound.

"I want every Zoe Pound member extinct. None of their bloodline should be breathing. Not a kid, mother, aunt, sister, grandmother, father, brother, or their fucking pet! Tell everyone I said spill blood all over Miami," Savage snarled with a menacing stare.

"No problem, homie. I'm sure the youngins is already on it. The death of Dirty Red is enough to raise the body count. I'm out of here. I need some rest. I'll see you tomorrow. Inshallah," Big Art said as he got up to leave.

"I'm going to send some money to Red's family. He was a good kid with a lot of heart. He will be missed, and we will triple his body count," Savage said as he began to make his salat.

Once Big Art departed and was halfway down the block, he spotted a black Impala with tints that stood out from the rest of the vehicles parked on the street. He tried to see who was in it, but had no luck.

Big Art continued to drive home, shrugging it off, which would turn out to be a mistake down the line.

Lil Snoop was riding around all night through the Miami hoods, looking for any Zoe Pound member he could smash to relieve some of the pain for his friend's death.

Lil Snoop was riding past the BP gas station when he thought he saw the black Taurus with bullet holes in the window, which looked like the same car from earlier. The 3 o'clock Miami morning air would bring you across strange things, especially when you were expecting those to either be long gone or in hiding.

Lil Snoop remembered the driver's face once he saw him pumping the gas.

This nigga has to be the dumbest nigga in the world to be riding around in a bullet riddled car, Lil Snoop thought as a devilish grin spread across his face.

Lil Snoop was about to call Big Art or Savage, but instead he pulled over so he'd be unnoticed. Lil Snoop didn't want to blow his cover.

Crazy Ra hopped back in the car without a care in the world, after he was done pumping gas. They'd been out all night. Big Moe was halfway asleep in the passenger seat.

"Where you heading to, Moe?" Crazy Ra asked, pulling off. "I'ma drop you off and go burn the car in the woods down the block from my house, so it don't come back to us," Crazy Ra informed.

"Take me home, because chopping two niggas up wasn't in my plans. It wore me out, cuz," Big Moe stated. "But it's about to be a lot of that. Our next target is Big Zoe's bitch ass! We going to get that nigga good." Big Moe plastered a wicked smile across his face.

Crazy Ra thought his cousin was tripping.

"We who?" Crazy Ra asked. "Moe, I'm not a killer. I'm just a driver. My reason for helping you was because I needed the money to feed my newborn. I don't want no problems with the Zoe Pound niggas. Plus, you work for him. Mind you, you're his best friend. Make me understand why you would turn against your man?" Crazy Ra said, driving through the Miami streets.

"Nigga, I work for myself. Remember that. And drop me off around the corner," scoffed Big Zoe.

Crazy Ra did as he was told, feeling like a bitch.

"Call Two-Five and Solo and have them niggas put me a team together tomorrow," Big Moe said before hopping out of the car and heading towards his apartment.

Once Crazy Ra pulled off, Lil Snoop hopped out of his car and made his way directly towards Big Moe's crib.

He'd followed them from the BP and now he was about 20 feet behind Big Moe.

Big Moe entered his crib slowly, as if he was drunk or tired. But as soon as he closed his door behind him, a hard force pushed it open, knocking him down to the floor.

Big Moe went to pull his gun, but it was a delayed reaction. Lil Snoop had beat him to the punch. His gun was already drawn and pointed between Big Moe's eyes.

Big Moe, seeing the face of Lil Snoop, knew he was caught slipping. A bright smile appeared on Lil Snoop's face. He almost laughed at the sight of Big Moe's facial expression, which was drenched in fear.

"Please, don't hurt me or my family. Take whatever," Big Moe said.

Lil Snoop laughed before saying, "Why does every bitch nigga say that?" It was more of a statement than a question.

Lil Snoop wasted no time tying up Big Moe before someone came into the foyer.

Lil Snoop was always prepared, due to him and Dirty Red always having to kidnap a person, so he pulled out two pairs of handcuffs. He cuffed Big Moe's hands and feet together while he laid on his stomach, looking like he was doing Yoga.

Lil Snoop walked calmly to the back and woke his wife and daughter, bringing them to the living room. Both were half asleep and very scared.

Once they saw Moe on the floor, crying like a baby, they both began to cry like babies. Lil Snoop pushed them both onto the floor next to him.

Big Moe's wife, Jordin, was a beautiful Puerto Rican woman with long jet-black hair. Their daughter was the spitting image of her mother, thank God.

Lil Snoop noticed the look in the female's eyes, as if he was about to touch her. She tried to fold the front of her thin robe around her thick body.

"I'm not into raping bitches, mami, so please don't flatter yourself," spat Lil Snoop.

Moe's daughter was crying for her daddy, while he was helpless and crying more than them both.

Lil Snoop walked over to the little girl, and aimed his gun at her head.

Boc.

Her brains splattered on her parents, as well as the chinchilla rug.

"Noooo," Jordin screamed as she went to lift her daughter's lifeless body off the floor as if she was asleep and she was going to put her in the bed.

Big Moe was speechless as he silently cried. He never realized he was going against the savages. Lil Snoop laughed, then turned the gun on Jordin.

Boc. Boc. Two shots welcomed themselves into her face, sending her right eye through the back of her head.

Lil Snoop's laugh was a horrifying one. It made Big Moe piss himself.

Big Moe watched Lil Snoop walk over to his wife's dead corpse and bend down. He put his fingers in her pussy. Lil Snoop looked at Big Moe as he licked his fingers.

"Damn, your wife taste good. I bet you're going to miss eating that pussy."

Lil Snoop walked over to Big Moe and shot him three times in his chest. Lil Snoop wiped down all of his prints, and then left the apartment as if he'd never come in. He had a bright smile on his face, knowing his best friend could now rest in peace with his killer.

***

Hours later, Savage and Gangsta Ock walked into an abandoned building in Jacksonville to attend to Super.

Savage wasn't in the mood to deal with any bullshit. He had Zoe Pound on his mind. They made their way to the backroom, where Lil Snoop and two soldiers were beating the hell out of Super with bats, bricks, and pistols.

All of their fun and laughter was interrupted once Savage walked in with a look that spoke volumes. They all fell back and left the room, with blood all over their clothes.

Lil Snoop was smiling, which made Savage wonder if he was okay after all that had been going on.

"Yo, you good, Lil Snoop? I'm sorry about Dirty Red. He'll be missed, and I mailed 200k out to his family," Savage said.

Gangsta Ock felt the young boy's pain, so he spoke up.

"We're going to find the killer," Gangsta Ock said proudly.

"No need for that. I killed him last night, along with his whole family," Lil Snoop replied nonchalantly. "What are we going to do with this bitch?" Lil Snoop growled, pointing at Super.

Savage and Gangsta Ock had no clue Lil Snoop was a cold hearted nigga like that, but they'd heard stories about the young man from Lil Shooter. They were both believers now.

Savage walked up to Super and spit in his face, while Super was drenched in fear.

"Well, well, well, Mr. Super, surprised to see you, my man. Where is Killer at? I'm sure he's not as dead as you." Savage's tone was that of ice.

Super face was swollen. He looked like he'd had plastic surgery that went wrong. Blood was everywhere, making it look worse.

"Savage," he spoke with a lisp, due to his teeth being knocked out and lips being swollen. "I swear, I haven't saw nor heard from Killer MPM in over three years. I changed my life. I'm saved now, and I have a family," Super pleaded, with tears running down his face.

"That's good to hear, but that's not what I want to hear, Super. So, I'm going to give you one more shot to get it right," Savage said in a calm tone.

Super started to cry as he begged Savage to spare his life. "I swear, Savage, I have no clue to his whereabouts. Come on, man, I would've just told you after what he did to me," Super said.

Savage pulled out his 357 and shot Super six times in the head. Then he walked out as if he didn't just kill a man. But in Savage's mind, Super was wasting his time.

Romell Tukes

Chapter 13

Stone was driving through his city in a candy red Benz Coupe with tinted windows, getting his dick sucked by a caramel complexion thick stripper from Sin City named Cinnamon.

Driving past Soundview Projects, he noticed flashing lights behind him, but Stone thought about bussing his nut in Cinnamon's mouth before pulling over.

Stone pushed Cinnamon's head deeper into his lap as she put his dick so far down her throat that her eyes got watery.

"Damn, girl," Stone squealed as he erupted in her mouth.

Cinnamon swallowed everything except for the cum that was dripping down the side of her mouth.

"Pick your head up, bitch, and clean your face," Stone said as he pulled over to the curb.

Cinnamon was embarrassed. All she could do was grab some napkins and shake her head.

Once the officer who pulled them over made it to the driver's window, he didn't give Stone a chance to speak.

"Where's my money? And I hope you got a good answer because the murder rate in the Bronx has been awfully high lately, with this darn Brim and Stones beef. Not to mention, your name is mentioned in every murder, shooting, and robbery," Sgt. Johnson said with a smirk.

"Look here, homie, I'll have your money dropped off to you tonight. I'll add a bonus, blood. Now can I go, because I got shit to do," Stone said as he rolled up his window.

Sgt. Raymond Johnson was a low life crooked cop who came up through the ranks by planting drugs and guns on dealers.

Stone dealt with him because he kept him and his homies out of prison.

Sgt. Johnson was from the Soundview Projects. He was an original Blood member of the Sex-Money-Murder set, which was the only reason Stone did business with him.

Stone was feeling that Johnson was light weight extorting him, so he had a little plan for the so-called homie. Stone was about to pull off until he saw a 305 area code flash across his phone. He had a feeling of who it was before he answered.

"What's popping? Who am I speaking to?" Stone said as he put his caller on speaker, pulling off.

"This Big Zoe, we gotta link up. How fast can you fly out with some good men?" Big Zoe questioned.

Stone knew off rip what Big Zoe was referring to, and it gave him a hard on.

"I'll be down there in a couple days. I'll call you as soon as I land," Stone said before hanging up.

Stone pulled over at a gas station on Gun Hill Rd.

"Cinnamon, I gotta go across the bridge. I'll call you later," Stone told her.

As soon as she was about to protest, Stone got out of the car, walked over to the passenger side, and opened the door.

He pulled her out and tossed her onto the ground with her purse.

"Bitch, I was trying to be nice to your stink pussy ass," Stone yelled in front of a crowd as he tossed her a couple dollars before hopping back into his car and pulling off, leaving behind a crying Cinnamon.

An hour later, Stone pulled up to the Lincoln Projects in Harlem to pick up some money, and to inform his goons about their road trip. As soon as Stone double parked his car, he walked into the first building, where there were at least thirty young boys dressed in red designer clothing, shooting dice and drinking.

"What's popping, Loco, Spayhoe, Dee, Ju, Pol, G-6. I see y'all out here losing all y'all re-up money," Stone said with a chuckle.

"Naw, blood, this only sixteen g's on the ground. I tossed that in Sue's last Tuesday," Spayhoe said as he released the dice and they crashed against the wall. "Tracy! Bitch, I hate when I head crack." Spayhoe shook his head then looked at Stone. "What brings you out here, boss, besides the pickup?" Spayhoe asked with a raised eyebrow as the two walked away from the dice game.

"Shawty about to drop that 150k in your truck as we speak," Spayhoe informed.

Stone looked towards his car to see a young lady in a dress with heels walking over to his car with two duffle bags.

"That's why I fuck with you, homie, but I'm also here trying to let you know I'm heading out to Miami in a couple days, and I need some soldiers," Stone told his homie.

"How many you talking? You know we all be out here trying to get it family," Spayhoe said while flashing money from the dice game.

"I know. That's why it's money for you niggas, and y'all can hit some clubs, fuck some bad bitches, but we're going down there to put in work, blood," Stone spoke with a serious tone.

"Stone, you know that's all we do around here, fam, so I'm going to holla at Loco, Tango, Turf, and Black," Spayhoe said. "They're on their way to Queens to put some work in as we speak," Spayhoe chuckled.

"Damn! Hit them nigga's and tell them to abort whatever mission it is. We have bigger business out in Miami. I'ma have Spazz, JB, and Davell come through to drop that work off later," he said, giving Spayhoe their signature handshake. "Oh, also, tell Tango Sgt. Hoe is dogfood," Stone stated in a tone that Spayhoe knew was to be taken seriously as he walked away.

Chapter 14

Britt waited for Savage to come home because she had set up a candle light dinner. Lately, things had been so busy for her, with school, the salon, and Lil Smoke, that she forgot about her husband's needs.

Britt also wanted to know what had her husband's spirits down lately, and had him out of the house so much. Britt was wearing a white mini dress that smothered her thick curves with a pair of high heels to match. She sat on the couch in their living room, drinking a glass of wine.

Savage walked into the house with four duffle bags as the seafood attacked his nostrils. As soon as he passed the dark living room, he looked to his left, where he saw his beautiful wife sitting down with her legs crossed, sipping on her wine.

"Damn, baby, why you in the dark?" Savage said, turning on the lights. He looked her up and down in amazement.

"I can't look good for my husband? I was waiting for you so we can spend some quality time together," Britt said, standing to her feet as she put her arms around Savage.

"Britt, I'm sorry I haven't been spending time with you or fulfilling my husband duties, but shit been crazy. I haven't even been able to spend time with Lil Smoke." Savage shook his head, feeling bad.

"What's wrong baby? I'm here for you. I know you don't want me involved in that type of life anymore, but just let me know for safety reasons," Britt said as she began to rub his shoulders.

"Okay, I'll fill you in, but I'm sweaty and I wanna take a shower and make love to my wife," Savage smiled.

"Good. I just took our food out the oven," Britt said, sashaying her way over to the kitchen with half her ass hanging from the bottom of her extremely short dress.

Savage followed his wife to the kitchen, amazed at how big her ass had gotten lately, and how it was hanging out, looking crazy.

Once they took their seats and started eating their seafood platter, Savage was pleased. Britt stopped eating and looked Savage in his eyes.

"So are you going to tell me what's up or stuff your handsome face, baby?" Britt smiled.

"Well, since it's safety reasons, we're at war with the Zoe Pound because I killed Sam, my connect, who JoJo put me on with," Savage said calmly, as if it was nothing.

Britt was somewhat surprised because she had no clue Savage would kill a person who he could benefit from, not to mention his own connect.

"Sam killed my father in New York a couple years back. He told me inadvertently, so I had to kill him before he killed me," Savage revealed. "He was a connected man, and now the Zoe Pound got a tip it was me that killed him and they been coming hard," Savage said. "I just hope I don't have to kill Jada because her baby's father is the head nigga we looking for, but she was a childhood friend to us," Savage stated.

Britt kept a poker face, though the mentioning of Jada's name made her insides boil and turned her stomach.

"I hate that crackhead, bitch," Britt spoke loudly. *I wish they would try to take my love away*. Britt thought to herself. She'd heard enough. She didn't want to talk about Jada or Zoe Pound any longer. Britt just wanted to make love to her husband.

"Can we go upstairs, baby?" Britt asked in a seductive tone.

Savage nodded his head and followed Britt upstairs to their bedroom. Once they made it behind closed doors, Savage laid Britt on the bed, hiking up her dress past her hips. He wasted no time allowing his tongue to swipe her moist fold as he pushed his tongue inside her love tunnel.

Britt closed her eyes tightly as her husband's tongue glided in and out of her.

"Ooooh, mmmy," Her words got stuck in her throat as Savage nibbled on her clit. Lost in her own sexual bliss, Britt bit down on her bottom lip as her clit swelled and she could no longer hold back from the way Savage magically worked his tongue.

"I-I-I'm cummming," she shouted, causing Savage to suck ever so gently on her clit as she released her sweet honey into his mouth.

Britt's legs shook uncontrollably as her body stiffened.

It was now Britt's turn as she took her husband into her watery mouth. The two switched positions all night. They made love into the wee hours.

***

Across town, Jada's thoughts were on Savage as she rode Big Zoe's stubby dick.

"Fuck that dick, baby," was all Big Zoe was shouting while Jada tried desperately to keep his little dick inside her wet pussy, and not to laugh.

Jada couldn't even get a nut with him. She was fed up with Big Zoe. Not only was his sex game trash, but he was too controlling, a cheater, ugly, and smelled like cow shit.

Jada hopped off his dick, once he came, in less than two minutes. No less than thirty seconds later, Big Zoe was sound asleep.

Jada did her normal routine by going to clean herself before heading to her Facebook page to look at Savage and get her nut off.

***

Shea and Gangsta Ock were making love for at least two hours straight, without a break. They were both tired and sweating like basketball players.

"Baby, your sex game is crazy," Gangsta Ock confessed with a smile. "I know you have niggas waiting in the bushes at your crib for you. Shit, if I wasn't Gangsta Ock, I'd be in them damn bushes waiting with them niggas!"

She laughed as she playfully smacked him. "Shut up, boy."

Shea knew she had some good pussy. Gangsta Ock was the only man she ever met that gave her a run for her money in the bedroom.

Her last boyfriend used to put his hands on her daily. Once her brother found out, he came up missing and Sheamika never heard from him again.

Shea stared at Gangsta Ock for what seemed like eternity.

"What's wrong?" He caressed the side of her face.

"I beg you not to hurt me. I truly like you and I want to be all yours," Shea told him with sincerity in her tone, as well as her eyes. "I know you're doing God knows what, but I can't be without you. I don't know what to do except ride with you." She revealed her true feelings as she laid in his muscular arms. "My last boyfriend abused me, and then my brother, Zoe Fresh, ran him away. But I'm sure you're a keeper." Shea smiled as she went under the covers attacking his penis.

Lost in total thought, Gangsta Ock knew he'd heard the name Zoe Fresh, but where? He knew it sounded familiar, but the way Shea was sucking the life out of him, he would have to come back to it.

Shea made sure she massaged his balls as she deep throated Gangsta Ock like a champ. Pre-cum oozed out of his penis. She slurped it up like a vacuum as her head bobbed up and down, causing Gangsta Ock's toes to curl. She sucked him until she got lock jaw.

The two fell asleep. Shea, thinking about her new lover, and Gangsta Ock with his mind on the name Zoe Fresh.

Chapter 15

Papi Goya was hands down the largest Colombian drug dealer in the South and Midwest. He built an empire that the Mexican Cartel could never create because so many Mexicans were killing each other or getting caught at the border. Papi Goya grew up in the capital of Colombia, which is Bogota. His parents were very wealthy, one of the richest families in Bogota.

His father, El Loco, was born in Havana, Cuba. His wife was born and raised in Colombia.

When El Loco and Papi Goya's mother met, he was just a worker for her, until he started to fuck her. His own connect, who was putting pleasure before business, eventually became pregnant, causing things to become worse for Marie Lopez, who was the Queen of Colombia. She'd made millions of dollars every day for over twenty plus years.

The second year after the birth of their baby, El Loco was killed by Marie's brother, Choco. A couple of days later, Marie met her untimely death, after being robbed for tons of cocaine and millions of dollars by her own brother.

Lil Goya was sent to Miami to stay with his father's brother as a child. Once Goya turned eighteen, he started traveling back and forth between Columbia and the US, just to hang out with his cousin, whom he'd reconnected with.

Goya had a connect, which was his cousin, Monkey, who had Columbia on lock on the drug tip. Once he put Goya on, there was no turning back. As years passed, Goya became a drug lord and JoJo was a friend he took a liking to. Goya recognized the Scarface mindset in JoJo, who moved weight like bodybuilding.

Recently, JoJo had given Papi Goya a call to have a sit down with a friend of his. Reluctantly, Papi Goya agreed to the sit down, and invited him and his company to his mansion in Key West, Florida.

***

It was the day of the meeting. JoJo and Savage were on time, actually a half-hour early. Once they arrived at the gated fortress, both men were impressed at the huge home with a massive lake on the side. There was heavy security, as if Papi Goya was the president.

Once they drove through the security check points, they had to go through a few more check points before being led to the conference room, where Papi Goya awaited them.

When they entered the room, Savage saw a man of a dark bronze complexion, with salt and pepper hair that was slicked back.

Papi Goya was in his mid-fifties, with a young face and dark black eyes that matched the color of train smoke.

His navy suit fit snugly on his broad shoulders as he eyed both men, especially Savage, who was dressed like a highly qualified executive.

"Good morning," Papi Goya spoke in an American voice. It surprised Savage, who thought he would have a thick accent.

Papi Goya looked at his Hublot watch as he smiled within.

"I see you two gentlemen are a half-hour early, which is good business in my eyes." He stood as he greeted JoJo, and then Savage.

"Papi Goya, this is Savage."

"Please sit." Papi Goya pointed to the empty seats.

"Are you sure you don't want a drink?" Papi Goya asked again.

"No, thank you. I prefer to do business." Savage got straight to the point, declining a drink.

Papi Goya shook his head. This was always a test he gave people he first met to see where their head was at, and Savage passed.

"Papi Goya, this here good man is my brother-in-law."

Papi Goya's facial expression slightly gave off a surprised look. He hoped that neither man noticed. What he didn't notice was that Savage was very observant, just how Papi Goya was, and he laughed inside when JoJo revealed that he was his brother-in-law.

"How can I be of service?" Papi Goya finally asked, over the initial shock.

"My brother here wants a new server to his line. I am no longer in that line of business. When I was, I hooked him up with Sam. But unfortunately, Sam is no longer in the physical," JoJo stated with a frown.

"Savage, you've done some good work," Papi Goya spoke as a wicked grin appeared.

Savage was a little confused the way the old man was looking at him.

Damn! I know he know something, Savage thought, keeping his poker face as he always did.

"You've done some great work as far as controlling your areas and staying off the FBI radar. I've done my research," Papi informed.

Savage was a little relieved to know that it wasn't about Sam's murder.

"JoJo, I love you as if you're my own son, so I'm going to work with your brother-in-law. Plus, I like him already," Papi Goya said with a smile. Papi Goya's smile quickly vanished as his face grew serious, staring directly in the eyes of Savage.

"Savage, I know you're smart, young, and dangerous, so this is why I will say never bite the hand that feeds you. Humans only have two hands, so when you bite one, how could the other one trust you?" It was more of a statement than a question.

Savage understood his meaning as he looked Papi Goya in the eyes.

"Thanks for the jewel, but you have my word and trust, because that is all I have as a man," Savage said profoundly.

"I hope so, young man. I will contact you tomorrow when your shipment arrives," Papi Goya said.

"Okay. Do you need my number?" Savage asked.

"That won't be necessary. I have your numbers and all three of your addresses, as well as your close friends," Papi Goya smiled.

Savage didn't want to look surprised, which he was, but his facial expression never changed.

"You have to know who you're dealing with, Savage. It's a dangerous game. JoJo is lucky he saw the good side and washed his hands before it was too late," explained Papi Goya. "Enjoy y'all day. I have a meeting in Vegas in 4 hours. Be safe and I'll be in touch." The old man said before getting up, exiting his conference room.

***

Big Art and Gangsta Ock was at a restaurant enjoying their evening with two beautiful women. Shea brought her friend from college for a double date.

Meka was a college student that had plans on becoming one of the best lawyers in Miami in another year.

"So, Meka, what's your plans after college?" Big Art asked her.

"My plan is to get people out of jail at a price people could afford." Meka smiled.

"That's great. We need more black female lawyers in American because our community is growing helpless. It has a lot to do with education," Big Art said, trying to sound educated.

Meka agreed with everything Big Art said. She was feeling him a lot, in his suit with his long dreads and blue eyes. Meka hated dealing with thirsty young niggas because she was on a different level. She was looking for a man, not a fuck, which she could do herself if needed.

Shea was sitting next to her friend peeping the vibe between Meka and Art. She was happy for her friend.

The women excused themselves to go use the restroom.

Gangsta Ock looked at Big Art.

"Yo, do you know who Zoe Fresh is?" Gangsta Ock asked.

"Yeah, that's Big Zoe's hitman, and half of Miami if the price is right. Word is, he's like a ghost when he comes for you, and he's deadly. Why you ask?" Big Art questioned with a raised eyebrow.

Gangsta Ock was pissed because he was in bed with the enemy's sister. No wonder the name sounded so familiar to him.

Big Art was about to ask him what the problem was, but Meka and Shea came back.

"Let's get out of here and go have a drink, then whatever after that," Meka said while locking eyes with Big Art.

Once they left the restaurant, they were all unaware that Zoe Fresh was on their tail, following them. But unbeknownst to Zoe Fresh, Lil Snoop and Lil Shooter were on his trail.

***

Back in New York, Brisco looked down at the paper with the address that was written on it.

The Suburban area had nice houses on manicured lawns. Brisco knew he didn't want to be caught in Mount Vernon, at this time of night, especially in this area.

Grabbing the large pizza box from the passenger seat, he excited his Domino's Pizza car, with the logo on the side, and walked to the beautiful brick home.

Brisco walked to the door, pushed the doorbell, and waited for it to be answered. The door swung open and a man stood shirtless, as if he'd just gotten out of the shower.

"Did you order pizza?"

"Nah, you have the wrong house," the man said, closing the door.

"Wait," Brisco called out.

"Yeah?"

"This isn't," Brisco paused. "Give me a second." He reached to his back pocket and, with lightning speed, lifted his arm, taking aim dead center of the face. The man froze, only to hear the .44 colt blast that knocked a chunk of his face off as his body dropped.

Sgt. Johnson was dead before he hit the floor as Brisco stood over him and emptied his chamber.

Brisco dropped the empty pizza box, calmly walked back to the car, and drove away.

Chapter 16

Zoe Fresh followed Gangsta Ock and Shea to the apartment complex in North Miami.

Zoe Fresh was glad the other couple went a separate way after their date because this made it much easier for him to make his move.

He was angry at himself because out of all people, his sister was hanging with, or maybe even fucking, his target. Zoe Fresh took his job seriously. Killing was like a drug to him, if he didn't kill, then he felt dope-sick and weak.

Lil Snoop and Lil Shooter were parked a couple blocks behind Zoe Fresh at Gangsta Ock's crib. They passed each other a blunt as their eyes fell on the police cruiser that rolled by.

"Let's make a move before he do, folk. I'm pretty sure the homie got cameras in his building, and we don't need to be seen," Lil Snoop explained.

"Nigga, I should be telling you this shit. You just came off the porch, I been in the field. Let me show you how it's done," Lil Shooter said as the two men hopped out of the hooptie with all black on, in August. They looked like Batman and Robin creeping through the dark streets.

Zoe Fresh was in deep thought as he watched Gangsta Ock and his sister walk into his building. Unbeknownst to Shea, Zoe Fresh had a GPS placed in her phone for many reasons, such as this one. The app made it all so good for him.

Zoe Fresh was planning ways to kill Gangsta Ock, without his sister getting involved. As soon as he came up with the perfect plan, we would eliminate Gangsta Ock.

He was taken away from his thoughts due to hearing something that startled him. As soon as Zoe Fresh turned to his left, he noticed a figure with dreads outside of his car, aiming a gun directly in his face.

"What is this all about, my brother?" Zoe Fresh asked. The nervousness in his voice could be detected as he tried to reach for his gun on his passenger seat as easily as he could.

Unbeknownst to Zoe Fresh, Lil Snoop was at the passenger side window with his .347 pointed at Zoe Fresh.

"I wouldn't do that if I was you, folk." The voice of Lil Snoop startled Zoe Fresh.

Zoe Fresh knew what time it was, so he decided to try and be diplomatic in a tough way.

"Listen, this is just the beginning. Y'all out of your league, homie. Zoe Pound will kill your whole family," Zoe Fresh said with a slight chuckle.

Lil Shooter smiled before saying, "This is how you choose to speak your last words? Well from one killer to an ex-killer, I'll see you in hell," Lil Shooter said before putting six bullets in his face.

Both Lil Shooter and Lil Snoop ran off and hopped in the car, making a clean getaway into the night air.

***

Big Art never brought a female to his crib. He would take them all to hotels or the back of one of his cars or trucks. Big Art and Meka's acquaintance didn't take long as they hit his bedroom. Big Art bent Meka over the bed with her ass spread. She was screaming at the top of her lungs as Big Art delivered long fast strokes from the back.

Big Art made sure to push all ten inches inside her as she begged for more. Meka's pussy was so wet and good.

Meka felt the swelling of his dick head and knew he was about to nut, so she pulled him out, grabbed his dick and placed it in her mouth.

"Damn, bitch," Big Art grunted as Meka bobbed her head, looking up into his eyes and playing with his balls.

Big Art bussed off and Meka swallowed every drop as she continued to suck the skin off his dick.

With the way Meka performed, Big Art knew he was locking her down. His eyes rolled into the back of his head. His knees buckled.

The entire night, Big Art had Meka cumming left and right from all positions. She knew Big Art was a blessing. She laid in his arms, feeling happy and secure for once.

As soon as she dozed off, her phone began to ring continuously, forcing Meka to wake up to answer it.

"Hello," she answered with an attitude.

All Meka could hear were the loud sobs of a female's voice.

"Someone killed him."

It didn't take long for Meka to recognize Shea's voice.

"Who killed who, Shea?"

"My brother. He got killed outside of Gangsta Ock's house." Meka hung up and quickly got dressed.

Big Art heard Shea's voice loud and clear, so he also got up and started to dress. He was confused as to why Shea's brother was dead outside of his man's crib.

***

Stone arrived in Miami a couple of days later with a couple of his goons, ready for action and payback.

Tango couldn't believe all the pretty women Miami had to offer as they walked back and forth in tight shorts, sundresses, and tight jeans at the airport.

"Damn, blood, the bitches looking like video vixens," Tango said while winking his eye at a snow-bunny, walking past and smiling.

"Yo, blood, chill. We here for business. We can chase pussy after," Stone said with a serious face.

As they stood in front waiting on Big Zoe, Stone knew all five men he'd brought were down to kill for the set, but he also thought about them dying.

The crew saw a long white stretch Bentley Limousine pull up with big rims and tinted windows.

Big Zoe rolled his window down from the backseat and told the crew to get in. Everybody followed Stone.

The driver pulled off into traffic, with a limo full of killers.

"Good to see you and your men make it in on short notice," Big Zoe said.

"This is my crew, and I can ensure you they're all trustworthy and trained to kill," Stone said proudly.

"I hope so, men. I'm Big Zoe. I run the Zoe Pound and majority of the drug trade in Miami," Big Zoe said. "To cut to the chase, men, Lil Sam's father was one every important man out here. He raised me like his own," Big Zoe said emotionally.

"I've been on a manhunt for his murderer, and I found him. He's a young man named Savage," Big Zoe said.

"So let's go get him, so I can catch the next flight back to the city, B," Turf said.

"Only if it was that easy, my crew would've been did it," Big Zoe said. But truth be told, Big Zoe refused to lose his crew when he could use these niggas.

"Savage is in his twenties. He has a big crew in Miami and Jacksonville. They run heavy and are dangerous," Big Zoe said as he took a sip of Henny. "We're at war with these young killers. Please don't underestimate them. One of my best killers was murdered last night in his car by them," Big Zoe said with a disappointed look. "I'ma place a couple of you in Jacksonville, and the rest will come to Miami," Big Zoe said.

The crew looked at each other with a smile, knowing that this would be too easy.

"I already have y'all apartments, fake IDs and names, credit cards, clothes, and females, to make y'all stay comfortable," Big Zoe stated. "Also, after the mission is complete, I will have a mill for each of you, and 150k is a gift awaiting you in y'all apartments," Big Zoe said proudly. As if money was no issue, he tossed five million in a strip club.

Everybody seemed cheerful, except Stone. He felt as if it was too good to be true, but the truth would all come to light sooner or later.

Big Zoe passed folders full of photos of Savage and his crew to each of the men. Everybody saw the pictures of the young men with dreads and laughed.

"These niggas look like babies," Spayhoe said.

"This must be a joke. My lil niggas could've handled these young niggas," Tango said, while rubbing his waves.

Stone saw something in the crew's eyes that made him a little uneasy. He wasn't scared, he just felt it wasn't going to be an easy task.

"I could've sent in my Zoe Pounds, but we all are on the radar for murders and extorting the powerful, so the feds are watching my crew," Big Zoe said, lying.

"This won't make us hot, I hope. I just did a fed bid in West VA," Turf said.

"No. I have set up everything where as you six will be un-noticed and unheard of in Miami, so you guys are like ghosts," Big Zoe said.

Stone sat there in silence, figuring out that Big Zoe was using his crew as pawns. But he had his own plans.

Chapter 17

Savage and his crew were in their new meeting location at a warehouse in Carol City. The warehouse was heavily armed with security, and gunmen patrolling every angle of the warehouse. Savage had a security team with his family 24/7, just until the Zoe Pound shit cooled down.

"Well I'm glad we can all make it to sit down," Savage said, looking around the round wooden table. "It's time we focus as a team on strategies and the art of war," Savage said with a smile.

Everybody smiled because they all understood the tactics of war, but they didn't understand the main concept of a battle.

"On another note, we have a new connect. He dropped off a shipment that got the streets going crazy," Savage said.

"We got Miami and Villie on lock, young and old niggas down with us. We come up from nothing and still humble," Savage said.

"Whoever said you can't get money and beef lied because our stacks and body count is up all the way up," Savage said.

Savage fixed his tie on his Balmain suit and took off his Gucci shades. "I'm glad Zoe Fresh and Moe are out the pic, but we still have bigger fish lurking," Savage said, referring to Big Zoe.

"The fat nigga been too quiet, bruh. And a loud nigga is never really quiet, unless he scared, or got something up his sleeve," Savage said with a smirk.

"So please be on point. I want everybody to attend the training base for training this weekend," Savage said.

"Also, before we split, I got good news. Bama should be back in Miami soon to fight his appeal. We owe him a lot for this empire, as we owe ourselves," Savage said before leaving.

Almost out the door, Gangsta Ock turned around to holla at Lil Shooter and Snoop about something.

"Yo, Lil Shooter and Lil Snoop, how did y'all know Fresh was following me?" Gangsta Ock asked.

"Well, nigga, if you wasn't fucking his sister, the enemy would've never found us. But we found him first, so don't worry about owing us," Lil Snoop said with a laugh.

"What the fuck you mean, little nigga? I don't owe y'all shit," Gangsta Ock said angrily. In reality, he knew he fucked up and they saved his life. "I'ma fuck who I want. You got a problem?" Gangsta Ock asked.

Lil Snoop looked at the nigga as if he'd lost his fucking mind. "Nigga, who the fuck you talking to?" Lil Snoop said, getting in Gangsta Ock's face, ready to swing on him.

Lil Shooter stood between both men. He saw both men try to reach for their weapons. He would've loved to see a fist fight, but shooting each other was out of the question. They had enough enemies to shoot.

"Chill the fuck out. We're a family. The beef is not with us. We're supposed to save each other, and protect each other," Lil Shooter said, calming the men down.

Big Art came inside from walking Savage to his car to see his team ready to kill each other. He grabbed Gangsta Ock, while Lil Shooter grabbed Lil Snoop.

On the way back to Jacksonville, Lil Snoop rode in his Porsche truck with his main soldier, Trov, as his driver.

"I should've put a hollow in that fuck nigga. He got me fucked up. I should've let that Haitian clown kill his ass," Lil Snoop said, while smoking a blunt of haze.

Trov started to laugh because, when Lil Snoop got worked up about anything, he always talked fast and wanted to put a hollow in a nigga.

"What the fuck so funny, nigga?" Lil Snoop asked.

"Nothing, but what's popping for tonight? The homies want to go out," Trov said with a chuckle.

Trov wasn't only Lil Snoop's soldier, he was also his first cousin on his mom's side, but they were totally different. And Trov was only seventeen.

Trov was a loyal soldier, who just wanted to have fun, live his youthful life, and rep for his Piru Blood set.

"Take me to go check on the trap on Smith St. Then take me to Tora crib, but make sure all the PJs good," Lil Snoop said.

Tora was Lil Snoop's baby's mother, whom he loved dearly, but she and Trov hated each other. They'd even gone to the same high school before she was his Snoop's BM.

Trov knew when he walked in Tora's crib, it was no leaving or sneaking out that mu'fucka, unless he had a bomb strapped to him. And even then, he still had a 50/50 shot.

"Okay, I'ma go to the club with them Southside niggas. I even recruited over twenty new youngins I knew," Trov said proudly.

"We going to hit up Club Live and some new shit on Main St.," Trov said while pulling up on Smith St. to see a bunch of goons trapping, and all of them were gang members.

Lil Snoop hopped out to pick up two book bags, and then hopped back in the car, not even listening to Trov. He had pussy on his mind.

***

Hours later, Trov and a couple of his goons entered a local strip club in Villie, before heading to Club Play.

Trov and his team were looking like famous football stars. They all had on so much ice that it started to glow in the dark.

The strippers already knew it was the Southside niggas because Trov was the bossman on that side of town, and everybody knew he was a young star with a big bag.

Once they hit the VIP section, they bought out the bar for the night for the party goers. The strippers came over ten deep to the VIP and started popping pussy, while doing splits and getting naked.

Trov was throwing fifties and hundreds, fuck ones and fives. Trov was paying these women's bills and college tuition.

Trov was enjoying himself so much that all anyone could see were the diamonds in his grill shining from his smile, as three strippers gave him a lap dance, while kissing each other.

The DJ gave him and the Southside crew a shout out, flexing on the sour faces in the club.

Once "Racks on Racks" by Tyga came on, almost every stripper was in the VIP, popping hard.

The liquor and pills had Trov fucked up. He thought he was seeing double, but he continued to throw hundreds of big faces in the air. Even the club security and hustlers picked up a couple of hundreds in the corner.

Everybody was so caught up in the moment, nobody saw the two dudes in the corner posted on the wall like posters.

"Yo, Turf, them niggas look like they getting money, son," Black said with envy.

"Look at them other niggas, blood. They stopped throwing money once they walked in," Black said, while looking around the club.

"Yeah, I be knowing, B, but tonight will be their last night turning up until they turn up dead. Now let's go wait outside. I hope Lil Snoop show up," Turf said as they walked outside to the parking lot.

Turf and Black had been following Trov and Lil Snoop since Smith St, but Turf was upset Lil Snoop didn't show. At first, he thought Trov was Lil Snoop, but Trov was 6'2 and Lil Snoop was 5'7.

Trov was drunk and ready to leave. He had two sexy bisexual strippers ready to leave with him. They ran to the back to prepare to leave.

The strippers couldn't wait to find out how much money Trov was about to trick off on them.

As soon as they walked outside, it was like World War III. Shots were being fired left and right, dropping Diamond and Posin like a bag of potatoes, both headshots.

Trov grabbed his pistol and busted back. He saw three of his men laid out. He knew he had no win with AKs, but he still sent shots.

Trov looked to his left as he ducked behind a car to see three of his men take off running with fully loaded guns in their hands.

Black chased the crew down the street, letting off his AK like a madman.

Turf's gun was jammed. As soon as Trov saw him trying to fix it, he ran down on him, emptying five shots in his heart and killing him instantly.

Black saw his homie get gunned down so he had to think quickly as he saw Trov running his way, unaware he was lurking. Black ducked low so Trov could run past him and he could get the drop, because he heard sirens from a distance.

Trov ran to his red Benz with the red flags hanging from his rearview mirrors. As soon as Trov unlocked his doors, he felt cold steel on his fresh braids.

"What's popping? You thought you was free, son," Black said, as if he was asking.

"Not at all, blood," Trov said.

Black saw the red flags in Trov's car and he knew he was a blood member, but he couldn't let him slide, even though Black hated blood on blood wars.

"I see you blooded, but it's too late. You was on the wrong team," Black said before blowing his brains on his car windows and running off. The sirens could be heard closing in on him.

Chapter 18

The next day, Stone and Tango were waiting in Miami, wondering what had taken place the previous night, since Black and Turf's phones were off.

Tango just so happened to be watching Fox News, where he saw "Headline News" that told the story of a shooting outside of a strip club that left over six people dead.

When Tango saw a pic of his homie Turf's face as one of the people who died, he called Stone to inform him.

Stone was pissed when he saw his friend's photo come across the TV as an ex-felon from New York murdered in Jacksonville.

Stone was confused as to how he lost one of his most valuable men in a couple of days in Florida, so he came up with a new plan.

"We can't cry over spoiled milk, so we gotta come up with our own plan as if we was up top, because Big Zoe's plans will have us all killed."

Big Zoe walked in with three muscle men on his side, as if he was the president.

"I told you gentlemen what we are up against, but I have a location on Big Art's mother's house in Miami, so y'all should send a message to bring the bait out," Big Zoe said.

"I'm losing time and money trying to hunt down this Savage kid. Normally, he would have been history, but I'm sorry for your loss," Big Zoe said, leaving a folder on the table before he left his mansion.

Tango wasn't feeling this nigga at all, but whatever his homies wanted to do, he was down.

"Okay, we going to make that trip tonight," Stone said before going upstairs to shower up.

Jada was in the living room, waiting for Big Zoe to take her shopping, when she overheard men talking in loud voices. There was a door connected to the guest living room. Jada placed her ear on the door to be nosey. She heard Big Zoe and his crew with up north accents say they were going on a mission and they were going to get Savage.

Jada ran off to the kitchen when she heard footsteps. All she could think about was the whole conversation she'd just overheard.

***

Lil Snoop was sitting outside of Trov's projects with thirty goons, smoking, drinking, and pouring out Henny for their lost ones, Trov and Dirty Red.

Lil Snoop had been fucked up since his aunty told him what happened to his little cousin at the strip club.

When she called him crying at 3am, he already knew what it was. That night he had a funny feeling about something. He just wished he would've gone with him.

Today Lil Snoop wasn't on this side of town to chill or hang out, he needed some answers so he could sleep a little better. Once he saw Big S, his cousin's best friend, he headed his way.

"Big S, what's up? I need to holla at you," Lil Snoop said, pulling him away from the crowd. Everybody knew that when Lil Snoop was around something was going down, even though these were his projects. He just let his goons run them so he could lay low from the feds.

"Who was with my cousin in the club? Word on the streets is there was some niggas there that took off," Lil Snoop said firmly.

Big S worked for Lil Snoop, shit, the whole hood did. He was the connect and a serial murderer. Big S didn't want to go against him to save some niggas he barely knew. Plus, Trov was his best friend.

Big S looked as if he knew the question was coming.

"It's two of them left. It was three, but when they ran, a bullet hit one in the back of the head," Big S said.

"Here in building 354, the apartment number is 6H," Big S said. But before he could finish, Lil Snoop walked off towards the building with a bottle of Henny in his hand.

Big S followed because they were close. If he had to choose sides of his hood, it would be Lil Snoop because he'd raised him and Trov.

Once they made it inside the building, they were greeted by some youngins who worked for Big S.

They finally made it to the 6th floor after riding in silence all that could be heard was click, click...

Lil Snoop used his spare key to enter. He had spare keys to all of his traps in the Villie.

Once inside, a couple youngins were playing Xbox and laughing, as if it was just another day in the hood, until they saw Big S and Lil Snoop standing there. The room got silent real quick, and niggas started sweating.

"I'm glad everybody made it out safely the other night," Lil Snoop said in a regular voice as he took a seat on the couch next to one of the teens.

"Yeah, good looking for checking on us, big homie. That shit happened so fast, we was putting our gun game down until our shit jammed," said Pookie, lying so hard he even believed himself. In reality, he was the first to run.

"I'm sorry about Trov. He got killed so fast. Then the police pulled up," Pookie said, hoping they believed them.

Levi and Richard looked at Pookie as if he was talking himself into a grave. The look on Big S was so disappointed because Pookie was a money getter, but he knew not for long.

"Well every dog has their day," Lil Snoop said, getting up. He pulled out the Ruger and shot Pookie four times in the head.

Before the other two youngins tried to reach for their AKs on the floor, Big S put two shots in both of their heads, while Lil Snoop emptied his clip in both their bodies.

Lil Snoop wiped off the door knob and walked outside as if nothing happened, leaving ten bricks and five assault rifles in the crib.

Big S sent a text to the cleanup crew to get rid of the bodies.

"I'm about to head to the north, but did you see that new love and hip-hop? Tommy looking good, folk," Lil Snoop said as he walked off to hop on his bike.

***

Big Art and Savage was coming to the mosque to make an evening prayer, something they hadn't done in months.

"It's crazy how they had the drop on Trov and Dirty. I know Lil Snoop is hurting," Big Art said. He liked the young man's ambition.

After talking and praying, both men left the mosque. As Big Art pulled off into traffic, he heard his phone ring. He hated to drive and take calls, but when he saw it was a private call, he thought it was one of his homies from prison.

Savage was daydreaming about spending the weekend with Britt and Lil Smoke until he heard Big Art cursing like a madman, something he never did.

"If you fucking touch her, I'll kill you, bitch. I swear," Big Art said before he heard the dial tone.

Big Art had tears in his eyes. Savage knew it was serious now. He hoped it wasn't too late for whatever it was.

"They got my mom at her house," Big Art said sadly.

Savage knew they were only two miles away.

"You go through the front and fake a surrender and I'ma come through the back. Just focus," Savage said.

Once they got around the block, Big Art pulled over to let Savage out. Then he made his way to his mom, wondering how Big Zoe pulled this off.

Once he made it inside his mom's house, he saw five Zoe Pound members pointing guns at him, while his mom was tied to a chair naked.

Big Art shed a tear for his poor mother's life as she looked hopeless.

"Ayo, put your gun on the floor, son," Stone said while aiming his gun at his mom's forehead.

Big Art did as he was told, while trying to figure out who these niggas were. They didn't look nor talk like Haitians. He was a Haitian, so he knew they wasn't even Jamaicans.

Big Art figured they were from New York because he did a bid in Attica, PA, and there were a lot of up top niggas there. They all use to say "Yo son," or "B."

"What the fuck y'all want?" Big Art asked.

"It's a long story, but I'll summarize it for you, B. First your bitch ass crew killed my father, Sam, and then y'all killed my homie, Turf. Is there any more to say, bitch nigga?" Stone said as he began to walk closer to Art with his gun drawn.

Before anybody could react, two members of Zoe Pound that Big Zoe sent were both shot in the back of their necks, multiple times.

Stone ran to the nearest corner, while Loco got low like a duck, because nobody saw where the shots were coming from.

Big Art grabbed his gun and shot twice at Loco, barely missing him. Then Savage came out the back, catching Stone off guard.

Savage shot over five rounds at Stone, one bullet hitting him in his leg. Stone ran upstairs because he was out of bullets.

Savage went to help Big Art, once he saw Stone fly upstairs.

Once Loco saw Savage coming from his left side, he knew he was done, so he fired his last two bullets into Big Art's mom's chest, killing her instantly.

Savage shot Loco five times in the head, while Big Art ran to his mother and dropped to his knees, screaming.

Savage grabbed Big Art from the ground and dragged him out the house. As soon as they made it out, bullets came ringing out from the upstairs balcony.

Stone was on the roof, shooting his extra gun, which he always kept in his Timbs. He shot wildly, hoping to hit them. But he was in too much pain to focus on hitting his targets.

Savage and Big Art tried to make a run back to Big Art's truck, but bullets were flying from above them. Savage heard a silence, so he figured it was clear. He and Big Art ran full speed to the car, until he felt a sharp pain in his left arm.

Savage and Big Art were out of bullets, but they made it to the truck. As soon as they pulled off, their back windshield shattered.

Savage saw he got shot in his arm and was pissed, but he was glad to be alive. Big Art just drove like a madman.

Stone saw his last two shots did damage to Savage and the truck. That made him smile as he ran back downstairs and limped to his Audi A8, which was parked two blocks down.

He pulled off slowly as he saw eight police cars speeding past him in the opposite direction of where he'd just come from.

Romell Tukes

Chapter 19

Britt walked in the house with Lil Smoke by her side, smiling with Toys-R-Us bags in his little hands.

"Go upstairs and go prepare for dinner," Britt told Lil Smoke, once she saw extra security patrolling the house.

Britt walked towards the basement, where she knew Savage would be. Once she got past the five-man security team, she saw the whole crew in the basement, mad and disappointed.

"I swear, I'ma kill them niggas. They don't know who they fucking with. I swear to Allah," Big Art said with tears flowing down his face.

"Can I talk to you Savage?" Britt asked as she intruded on the men's emotional party.

Savage got up and walked to his wife to see why she had a concerned look.

"Baby, what's going on around here?" Britt said in a low voice.

"Well I'm not going to start lyin to you now, boo. You still part of the crew, but we got problems with the Zoe Pound. They just killed Big Art's mom, and I got hit in the arm," Savage said while pointing at his casted arm.

Britt was speechless, but had felt something was wrong for the past couple days. Her husband getting shot was too much to bear.

"I'ma move you and Lil Smoke tonight. I have a condo in Palm Beach we're staying at until shit dies down because it's about to get crazy," Savage said.

"You promised me we wouldn't go through this shit again," Britt said with glossy eyes.

"Here goes the address. Take Ms. Jackson with you. Plus, four of my men. Baby, I'm sorry," Savage said as he walked back in the room, leaving her upset.

Britt walked upstairs, pissed, but what Savage didn't know was that Britt had some plans of her own.

***

Big Zoe had a private doctor patching up Stone's leg in his guest room. Stone didn't know he was hit until he drove away from the shootout.

"I almost had them niggas, Zoe, until some dude with a icy grill and long dreads caught me slipping. Blood, they killed all our men. Who the fuck is that nigga?" Stone asked everybody in the room.

Big Zoe was mad he'd lost two of his best men. He didn't give a fuck about Stone or his crew.

"Take a guess," Big Zoe said as he got up and stared out the window.

"Well if that was Savage, at least I shot him. And Loco killed Big Art's mom before they killed him," Stone said.

Big Zoe was so busy putting a new plan together, he was deaf to what Stone was saying.

"Get it together. I got a plan for Jacksonville," Big Zoe said with a smirk.

Jada texted Savage asking if they could meet at the Hilton Hotel tonight because she had something very important to discuss.

Once he replied, "Ok," she got dressed in less than an hour. While looking at herself in the mirror in her Fendi mini skirt, she prayed the night went as she planned.

Jada went upstairs to check on her son before she left. Once she saw her child sleeping and the babysitter watching TV, she made her exit.

Jada was happy her beautiful child looked nothing like Big Zoe.

Jada was no dummy. She was updated on the news and the streets. She knew sooner or later Big Zoe would be a deadbeat, literally, and she would do anything to protect her son and her life.

As Jada was about to walk out of the house, Big Zoe walked in with a seven-man crew and Popeye's baskets full of chicken.

"Hey, baby, where you going dressed like that?" Big Zoe asked as he kissed her on the cheeks.

"Well, if you must know, I'm going to have a night out with the girls, big daddy," Jada said with a fake smile, hoping his fat ass would move from blocking her way out.

"I'ma send a team with you," Big Zoe said as he dialed a number.

"I'm not no fucking kid. I don't live your life, and I'm not living in fear. My son shouldn't have to either," Jada said in anger.

"I just want to make sure you safe, Jada. You have no clue what's going on," Big Zoe said, getting pissed.

Jada looked at him and laughed. Then she walked out the door, switching her wide hips and fat ass.

Big Zoe slammed the door, shaking his head. He was getting sick of Jada anyway. He'd just left his second wife, whose head game was amazing.

Jada pulled up to the fancy hotel in her navy blue Bentley Coupe, hoping to beat Savage there so she could set up the room to make it look sexy.

Savage pulled up minutes later in his all-white BMW 3 series by himself, no security. He hopped out, looking like a GQ model on the runway in New York City.

Savage saw Jada sitting in the lobby, wearing a beautiful tight French skirt and Chanel blouse, with some red bottom high heels on, looking like eye candy.

Once they hugged each other, Savage felt something wrong with Jada. She seemed a little nervous.

"I ordered us a room so we can talk in private," Jada said as she made her way upstairs with Savage on her heels.

Once in the room, Savage took a seat on the couch. He was checking out the roses, chocolate, and candles laid out everywhere.

"So, this what was so important?" Savage said with an attitude.

"No, Savage, I called you because I know what's going on Big Zoe is trying to kill you and he got some New York niggas down here trying to kill you," Jada said with tears.

Savage didn't know her angle, whether she was a friend or foe, but her emotions were real.

"Why are you telling me this?" Savage asked.

"Because I don't want to see you dead, or my child. My loyalty remains with you," Jada said.

"Jada, I will never hurt you or your child, but Zoe is a dead man. And I'ma kill him myself," Savage said sternly as he stood to leave.

Jada saw him about to leave, so she grabbed him and yelled, "Savage, I love you," with tears rolling down her pretty face.

"I need you. I can't live without you. And I owe my life to you, Savage. I know you married, but I can't control my love or feelings for you," Jada said.

Savage had to sit back down. He was blown away. He wondered if she was high or confused.

Savage wiped her tears away and hugged her until her cries stopped. Savage felt Jada's warm, soft, smooth body, and he felt his dick get hard.

Jada felt Savage's dick poke her pussy, making her pussy wet, and her mouth even wetter.

Savage was so caught up in the moment, he didn't see Jada drop to her knees.

Jada unbuckled his Balmain jeans to see two chrome pistols staring at her, but Savage slid his guns on the couch.

Jada pulled his jeans to his ankles while she climbed between his tatted up legs.

Savage wanted to push her away so bad, but it felt so good, and his dick was growing every second.

Jada grabbed his dick as if it was a prize. She was amazed at how long and fat it was.

Jada put her juicy wet lips on the tip, placing a kiss on the head of his penis. Jada began to suck the head and do tricks with her tongue.

Jada started to bop deeper, while spitting on it, making Savage ease back with pleasure. Once she started to deep throat him, she felt pre-cum dripping, so she played with the cum.

Savage felt himself about to cum, so he lifted Jada off the floor, while pulling her clothes off and admiring her sexy body. Savage took her to the master bedroom and laid her on the bed, spreading her legs like an eagle.

Jada pussy was so wet it was dripping. She had fat, soft, pretty lips that turned him on. Savage was sucking her phat clit, while fingering her wet love box, making her moan.

"Oh yessss, daddy. Suck my tight pussy. Yesss, I'm bout to cum, daddy," Jada yelled.

After three minutes of sucking, Jada was climaxing in Savage's mouth, while her legs were shaking uncontrollably.

Once Savage was done, he got on top of her in the missionary position. Savage felt how tight her pussy was and he almost came from one stroke.

Jada closed her eyes tightly as she got used to the pain of his massive dick. Once she got used to his dick, she was grabbing his ass so he could go deeper.

Savage came twice in her pussy while his dick was still hard. Jada was grabbing his dick with her tight walls, making him nut back to back. After two hours of love making, they both fell asleep, unaware of a real killer lurking in their shadow.

Chapter 20

Bama had just gotten off the phone with his little cousin, who was informing him how crazy Miami was getting with his crew.

It was no surprise to Bama because his lawyer told him the other day that Savage was laying low. Plus, Britt sent him five thousand dollars to his account, and wrote him a sentence saying everything was changing.

Bama prayed his friend would get out the game before it was too late because the streets were talking heavy, even in prison, about the boss.

In the next week or so, Bama would be back in Miami, fighting his appeal. With the grace of Allah, he would be given a second change.

Bama swore to never get caught up in the street life again. He hoped his new life as a Muslim would make him into a better man.

Bama had met a lot of smart, good men in the feds, from all over the country, even though USPs were full of lifers and the worst criminals in America.

Bama made his way to the library when they made an announcement for moves. As he made his way, he saw a lot of homies he spoke to.

Once in the library, he found the book he was looking for called "Destruction of Black Civilization" by a writer named Chancellor William.

Bama stood for something, not just a Muslim man, but "Redemption" because he'd found himself, and now was trying to help others.

Bama saw a bunch of gang members cursing and playing as if they were kids. He signed the book out and left because he had Arabic classes to teach to new Muslims.

***

Lil Shooter and Gangsta Ock were in Jacksonville at one of Lil Snoop projects. They were informing him to shut down all operations for the day.

"They supposed to come thru and make a move, so Savage wants us to be on point," Lil Shooter said to Lil Snoop.

"You see all this money coming in and out?" Lil Snoop asked, pointing at the fiends running around.

"Anyway, I'ma shut it down right now. But how is Big Art? Tell him I send my graces and love," Lil Snoop said as she walked off to tell his young workers to fall back for the day.

Hours later, Lil Snoop stood in front of another of his projects, chilling with his folks and the Pirus he grew up with.

The fiends knew it was dry for the day, so they all went across town to the Mexicans or went cold turkey for 24 hours.

Big S and Lil Snoop saw two funny looking fiends walking down the street, drinking a Cuban beer in 102 degree weather, with coats on.

The two dirty fiends approached Lil Snoop, asking him if he had any crack. Lil Snoop told the two fiends to, get the fuck out of his face.

As they made their way to the next building, pushing a cart full of cans, Lil Snoop and Big S knew something was wrong with the two fiends.

Big S knew every fiend around the area, but he'd never seen the two dirty fiends before.

"Yo, folk, you ever saw them around here?" Lil Snoop asked Big S.

"Naw, but it sounds like they from up north. I'm about to follow them in building 357," Big S said.

***

Thirty Minutes Earlier

Lil Shooter and Gangsta Ock were parked three blocks away from Lil Snoop and his young goons, because Savage ordered them to.

Gangsta Ock was eating Chinese food while listening to the OJs on the radio, while Lil Shooter watched the block for anything out of the ordinary.

"Yo, bruh, you see that shit?" Lil Shooter said while pointing at the two fiends getting out of the pearl white Bentley coupe, tucking their guns.

Once Big S entered the building, he saw nothing. He even checked the staircase, which was where he saw the two fiends with big guns pointed at him.

"What's popping? You fell right in my hands, big man," Black said with a smile.

Big S knew it was over, but he tried to reach for his gun anyway. Spayhoe deaded that when he blew his brains on the stairway walls.

Lil Shooter and Gangsta Ock were already in the building when they heard the loud boom. So they made their move.

Gangsta Ock came from the top of the staircase busting, hitting Black in the chest three times and causing him to lean over in slow motion before rolling down the stairs.

Once Spayhoe saw his homie die with his eyes open, he busted his desert eagle until he felt a burner to his head from behind, freezing him in his tracks.

Lil Shooter had his 357 to the back of Spayhoe's head with a smile on his face. Before Spayhoe could even get a word out, Lil Shooter put five bullets in his head.

Gangsta Ock walked down the stairs to leave, stepping over the dead bodies. When he reached the entrance, he saw Lil Snoop and his crew run into the building with their guns drawn.

Once Lil Snoop saw Big S dead body, and the two fiends beside him, he knew it was the hit.

Lil Snoop looked at his crew and Lil Shooter. Then he left the building before the police was called.

Chapter 21

Agent Nelson was the new chief of the FBI in Miami, since Agent Joseph was fired last year for lying on the stand, hiring false witnesses, and shooting an unarmed civilian.

"Due to all the murders and violence going on in Miami and Jacksonville, and our links to both cities, I called this meeting today," Nelson stated to the agents in the room.

"As you see on the screen, we have over ten dead bodies in the last week, thanks to Savage and the Zoe Pound," Agent Nelson said while pointing at the screen with everybody's picture on it.

"We have no solid evidence, gentlemen, as of yet, but we do have snitches in both circles that will be willing to testify," Agent Nelson said as he ended the meeting and walked towards his office.

Agent Nelson sat at his desk, thinking about Meka and the last time he tasted her sweet juices. Nelson was twenty-seven, no wife, no kids, and stable, with a lot of money. Plus, he was a handsome, Slim Shady lookalike. Agent Nelson loved black women. That was his dirty secret. He had jungle fever, so he called Meka for a booty call later that night.

***

Meka was on Spring Break from college, so she spent her time shopping, clubbing, and having sex with Big Art. She knew he needed her the most right now, since his mother's death, so she thought about putting school on hold for her boo.

Meka was falling hard for Big Art, but her past lover was always finding ways to creep back into the picture. The only reason why she was fucking with Nelson's lame ass was because he attended college with her. He was handsome and had been financial stable since she met him. Meka hated broke niggas.

Nelson was old news, and his sex was like fucking a rabbit with a small dick, she thought as she left the Gucci store.

Meka heard "Cheated" by Keyshia Cole playing through her phone. She answered, hoping it was her boo.

Once she heard the voice on the other end, she wished she would've never answered. Nelson asked her to come by for dinner and wine. He had something important to tell her.

Meka said yes. She had no plans and saw no harm in letting him know she'd found her true love, so she agreed to meet at his crib at seven.

Meka hopped in her pink LS Lexus and drove to the mall to get her nails and hair done for the night.

***

Hours Later

Meka pulled up behind Nelson's Audi R8, which was parked in his driveway. Meka hopped out of her car in her bright red Gucci slit dress, showing off her sexy, long legs and curvy body.

Nelson opened the door with a hard-on, looking amazing in his slacks and Michael Kors bottom up.

"You look amazing. It's been a while," Nelson said as he led her into his house, while staring at her fat ass.

Meka took a seat in the living room, while Nelson went in the kitchen to turn off the stove. Meka saw stacks of papers all over the table. She saw a lot of dead bodies and photos of Haitians. When Meka moved the photos, she saw a photo of Savage and Gangster Ock. But when she saw Big Art, her heart stopped.

Nelson walked back into the living room with two glasses of wine. He saw an odd look on Meka's face. When he saw his caseload, he figured the dead people shook her up.

"Sorry about that, Meka, I got a heavy caseload. But everything is set up in the kitchen," Nelson said, gathering all of his paperwork up to put in his folders.

Meka played cool. As she saw the rice, shrimp, fish, green beans, and candles lit, she laughed to herself.

"Yep, it's all for you. I really miss you and the way you taste," Nelson said as he took a seat next to her. Nelson didn't even take a bite of his food before he got up and started to rub her shoulders, making her uneasy.

"Nelson, I'm sorry, but I didn't come here for this at all," Meka said, getting up.

"What? So why did you wear that slutty dress? I know you want this dick, Meka. I can see it in your eyes. You want to suck it like you used to," Nelson said proudly.

"Nigga, you fucking tripping. I got a man. I'm not a whore, and you was a mistake," Meka said, pissed off.

"Meka, I miss you, and I need you. You can use a black 12-inch vibrator on me. That will be special. You're the only person I can explore my sex fantasies with," Nelson said.

Meka was at a loss for words. She knew he was a freak because, months ago, he begged her to put her finger and tongue in his ass.

"Nelson, what the fuck has gotten into you. I'm not into no gay shit," Meka yelled.

Nelson's face turned beet red. He was pissed because Meka was being a bitch, he thought.

"Forget I even asked you, bitch. Get the fuck outta my house, you ghetto thot," Nelson yelled.

Meka left without saying a word. She'd never felt so disrespected. She vowed Nelson would pay for the disrespect.

Once outside, Meka picked up the biggest brick she saw and busted back window out of his Audi R8.

Meka hopped in her car and pulled off laughing, with her windows down, driving to Big Art's condo.

Once at Big Art's crib, Meka used her key that she'd just recently received. Big Art was in the kitchen cooking, with two pistols and a Draco on the floor.

Meka ran up to Big Art, holding him with tears rolling and puffy, red eyes. Once Big Art asked what happened, she told him everything.

"I thought you left this lifestyle alone. You told me you had a business," Meka said with tears.

Big Art walked to the guest room and came out with big folders with business documents to prove that he did have businesses as well.

Big Art was surprised a rookie was on his crew's tail. He had Miami Vice on payroll, but the feds was priceless.

"Baby, did you tell him anything about me?" Big Art asked, looking at her.

"Baby, I love you, and I'm not a dummy. I'm with you until the end," Meka said.

Big Art kissed her on her soft lips, then made love to her until she fell asleep like a big baby.

Big Art went to take a shower to clear his mind because so much was going on with his mother's death, Zoe Pound, and now the feds.

Big Art came up with a plan while he washed his dreads, but his main source was Meka. He needed her loyalty. He was about see where her loyalty stood with him.

Chapter 22

Stone and Tango were the only two left out of their crew. They had no clue what they were up against when they got off the phone.

"I can't believe all the homies are dead, blood. We gotta remain rock solid and kill these fuck boys," Tango said as he reclined his seat in Stone's black Benz as they cruised through Miami streets.

"I feel you, blood, but Big Zoe got some new info. Hopefully it's the break," Stone said as he stopped at a red light on a four way.

Stone was staring out his window when he saw someone who caught his attention.

***

Gangsta Ock and Shea were both walking out of the Prada store on Collins Ave with bags as they tried to blend in with crowd.

Shea had been living with Gangsta Ock since her brother's death because she was scared and needed a man's affection and protection. Shea was in deep thought as she was about to cross the street.

"Baby, you're okay. It's a greenlight," Gangsta Ock said, while snapping her out of her zone.

"Oh, I'm sorry, boo. I was thinking about the surprise I had for you tonight," Shea said with a smile.

Once they made it to the car, their security team was on standby, trying their best to be unnoticed as they pulled off in the Hummer behind Gangsta Ock. But they were all unaware of the black Benz behind them, tailing them.

***

Britt was in Palm Beach at Savage's condo, making lunch for Lil Smoke, while Ms. Jackson went shopping for more food.

"Sis, can we go out today? Please, please, please," Lil Smoke shouted as he jumped up and down on the Versace couch.

"No, baby, it's too hot out. I don't want the sun to burn you," Britt said, bringing him his lunch.

"I got your favorite movies, Shrek, Pandora, and Ice Age," Britt said, hoping to change his mood.

Lil Smoke put his hand on his little chin as if he was in deep thought.

"Okay, sis, I wanna see Ice Age for the sixth time," Lil Smoke said.

Britt looked at him funny because she knew he was being a smart ass.

"Sis, when can we go back home? I think all the monsters are gone," Lil Smoke said with his hazel puppy dog eyes.

Britt told him the monster story so he wouldn't worry too much about why they moved from home.

"Oh, baby, they will be gone soon," Britt said as she put the movie on for him.

Britt walked toward her bedroom, where Savage was sleeping on the king size bed, with his dreads hanging off the bed.

Britt saw Savage's clothes all over the floor, so she picked them up. While folding his Balmain jeans, Savage's cell phone slipped out.

Britt never looked in his phone because she trusted her husband, but it kept ringing, as if it was an emergency. She took a peak and saw a 404 area code.

Britt wondered what business Savage had in Atlanta, so she read the text.

"Can I see you again, please? Your touch did something to me that I never felt. Please, I need you," was sent from an unknown person.

Britt felt tears and her heart froze. She loved Savage, but this was too much. She memorized the number and put his clothes where she found them.

When she walked back into the kitchen, Ms. Jackson acted as if she didn't even see Britt. She chose to mind her business, but she hated to see the beautiful woman in distress.

***

Gangsta Ock and Shea had just come back home from a diner and comedy show they'd attended downtown. Shea was looking amazing in her Herma dress, while Gangsta Ock wore his Armani suit.

Lately, he realized Shea had been eating a lot, but he thought it was the stress of her loss. Gangsta Ock felt it was no need for a security team outside his house 24/7, even though it was Savage's orders.

The couple took a shower together and made ice cream for the movie they were preparing to watch.

Stone and Tango had followed the security team around all day. Now they were parked a couple of cars behind them in a black Tahoe truck.

"Homie, I just saw the lights go off. Let's go do this," Stone said as he put his gloves and ski mask on.

Tango was smoking a blunt of wet PCP, while listening to Jadakiss. Tango was burnt, due to a house fire when he was kid, so half of his face and body had third degree burns, making him look pink and black.

Unfortunately for his parents, they were both killed from the fire he caused, so hurting people had become a high to him, after growing up in group homes.

Both men got out of the truck and walked towards the parked Chevy truck with two security guards inside, half asleep, listening to Waka Flocka's new album.

"Aye, Rell, wake up. We both can't be sleep. If Agent Nelson rolls up on us, we heading back to the desk. I hate that young, racist punk," Agent Watson said, waking Agent Rell up.

Tango and Stone had no clue these men were agents staking out Gangsta Ock and his crib. Savage's security team had left hours ago because Gangsta Ock told them to.

Tango and Stone walked right up on the agents' car and fired shots into the agents' faces and chests, with silencers on their Ruggers.

As Gangsta Ock and Shea sat down, Shea told him it was time for her surprise.

"Baby, I'm pregnant," Shea said happily.

"Oh shit, baby, yessssss," Gangsta Ock said. He hugged her softly with happy tears in his eyes. He always wanted a child.

Gangsta Ock went into the backroom to text Savage and Big Art the news, while Shea thought of his reaction and how happy and ready she was.

Gangsta Ock heard a loud boom, causing him to grab his pistol. But when he made it to the living room, he saw a young man pointing a gun at Shea's head, and an ugly nigga pointing a gun at him, smiling.

"Get next to your bitch. But first, drop your fucking gun," Tango said sternly.

Gangsta Ock wanted to shoot, but he knew his unborn child would be killed, so he did as he was told. He dropped his gun and held Shea, telling her it would be okay.

Tango was so sick of Shea's crying he started beating Gangsta Ock with his pistol, while telling her to shut up.

Stone slapped her with the pistol, shutting her up. As she laid there, her titties and clean shaved pussy were exposed, turning them enemy on.

Gangsta Ock was barely alive and awake from being pistol whipped for over twenty minutes. Tango's dick was so hard that he was sweating. As he stared at Shea's pretty private parts, he couldn't control himself.

"Take off your robe, bitch, and come here," Tango said to Shea with fire in his eyes.

Shea did as she was told. She had two guns pointed at her, and her lover was barely alive.

Tango pushed Shea on the couch and forced her legs open. He began to suck on her clit roughly, while taking off his clothes. Once he was naked, Tango forced his dick into her wet, tight pussy. It was so tight he had to force his way in.

Stone held Gangsta Ock at gunpoint, disgusted at his friend's behavior, but he let him vent.

"Oh my God, please stop. You're hurting me and my unborn baby," Shea said through her moans and cries.

Tango flipped her over and rammed his massive penis into her anus until he saw blood all over his shirt, legs, and his hands.

Gangsta Ock heard the moans and cries, but there was nothing he could do except cry for her.

"They going to kill you and your whole family," Gangsta Ock said, spitting out blood.

Stone's reply was three bullets to his head, killing him instantly.

When Tango was done raping Shea, he shot her three times in the stomach and once in the forehead. Then he smiled and told Stone that was best pussy he'd ever had.

Stone knew his friend had mental problems, but this was overboard.

Chapter 23

Two days later

Big Art and Lil Shooter were in a private location, discussing business with Savage about a new club they wanted to open, since they'd already bought the building. Savage had over six up and running businesses, from clothing stores, to bars, gas stations, and even a hair salon.

"Has anybody saw Gangsta? He was supposed to be here," Savage said.

"Naw, I just got a text the other night saying Shea was pregnant," Big Art said.

"I spoke to Lil Snoop. He was crushed about Big S funeral, but Gangsta Ock's phone been off. I've tried to reach out," Lil Shooter said while sipping Cîroc.

"Okay, I'ma handle it. But I got 200 bricks coming in from Papi, so I need everybody to be on deck tonight," Savage said.

"I forgot, we have a big problem. Meka's ex is the chief of the FBI, and he is on to us. Meka saw photos of us and dead bodies at his crib, but me and Lil Snoop going to handle that tonight," Big Art started.

"Okay, me and Lil Shooter going to break down the bricks to O-Town, Homestead, Parky, and Carol City tonight," Savage said with a cocky attitude.

***

Hours Later

Big Art walked into his apartment to see Meka sitting in the dark, watching CSI on TV and eating ice cream and cookies.

"Hey, boo, how was your day?" Meka said with crumbs around her face.

"I'm ok, but I need a big favor, boo," Big Art said in a sad voice.

Meka saw the worried look on his face, so she hoped she could help her lover.

"I need you to set Nelson up tonight," Big Art announced.

Meka looked at him and laughed. She said, "Hell yea," then continued to watch her show.

Big Art explained how serious this was, and he went over a plan he'd come up with days ago.

Meka called Nelson, apologized, and stroked his ego. Then she set up a date for that night at 7pm, and he was more than happy.

Meka arrived on time to Nelson's house. He answered the door shirtless with a smile, saying he'd just got done exercising. After an hour of talking about college days, politics, and his new position in the FBI, Nelson was horny and Meka was ready to kill herself.

Nelson dimmed the lights and rubbed on Meka's thighs as she opened them wider. Once he felt her wet, warm pussy, he was ready to eat it on the couch. Meka started to massage his manhood, turning him on. She had his soul in her hands.

"Let's go upstairs," Meka said as she pulled her dress down, showing her fat ass.

Meka rushed to unlock the door, then she walked upstairs.

When Meka entered his room, she saw candles, chains hanging, whips, metal balls, and long colorful dildos. She wanted to throw up.

Nelson was laying on the bed naked, with a pair of pink furry cuffs locked on his hands.

Meka got undressed and climbed in the bed to sit on his face. She rode his face until she came in his mouth. She hurried because this wasn't part of Big Art's plan, but she was a little horny.

"Meka, please don't tell nobody about my secret life. My career is on the line," Nelson said.

"Okay, daddy," Meka said as she blindfolded him and got off the bed.

"Open the drawer and get the black one," Nelson said with a grin.

Meka put her dress on and opened the drawer to see over twenty dildos lined up, and a black one that was over fourteen inches long.

"Did you find it, princess?" Nelson asked as he flipped on his stomach, wasting no time.

"Yes, daddy," Meka said in a dry voice, hoping Big Art would bust in. Meka got a scoop of Vaseline, feeling scared.

Meka put Vaseline on the tip of the dildo and rammed it in his ass. Nelson moaned as he took it like a champ.

"Go deeper, pleaseee. Oh yesss," Nelson moaned as Meka pushed the massive dildo until it couldn't go anymore.

Nelson was loving the way it felt. He was so caught up in his fantasy that he didn't even see three niggas with dreads and icy grills walk into the room masked up.

"That's enough of the freaky shit," Big Art said in a deep voice, fucking up Nelson's groove. Meka ran to the bathroom to wash Nelson off her hands.

Lil Snoop removed the blindfold from Nelson head, while pointing his Draco at his face and covering his noise, due to the foul smell.

Agent Nelson was hoping it would be an orgy, or something similar, but when he saw the biggest one pull off his mask, he shitted himself.

"How did you get in my house, you murderer?" Nelson yelled. But when he saw Meka shake her head, he knew it was a set up.

Before he could say another word, Lil Snoop, Big Art, and their solider fired over fifty rounds into his lifeless body.

Everybody looked at Meka, making her feel very uncomfortable. But when her man passed her the gun, she knew what she had to, so she emptied the clip in Nelson's body.

***

Savage pulled up to Gangsta Ock's crib with two trucks full of men behind his Bentley. He walked to the second floor, and smelled a strong odor that was too familiar. Once he walked into Gangsta Ock's apartment, the smell hit him even harder.

Savage was surprised his door was unlocked, but when he walked into the living room, he saw two dead bodies lying on top of each other.

Savage was pissed. He left their crib as if nothing happened and called a cleanup crew. He promised himself that Big Zoe would be a dead man before the weekend.

Chapter 24

Savage and Jada been creeping around lately. Savage never wanted to use Jada sexually, only for info to kill Big Zoe, but his plan going left.

Lately, Savage felt as if somebody was following him around, but he made himself believe he was just being paranoid.

Since two Agents were murdered on Gangsta Ock's block, police been on bullshit all over Miami, trying to find the killers. But Savage had first dibs.

Jada laid in the hotel, dripping sweat as if she'd just left the gym, Savage's gym.

The sex Savage gave her fucked her up mentally. It was so good that she was ready to go to war with North Korea for his dick.

"Why are you doing this? I'm addicted to you, and I need you," Jada said, covering her naked body in the silk sheets. Savage sat on the edge of the bed, ready to take a shower and head home, but Jada was falling in love. He had to be real with himself.

"Jada, I like you, and the sex was amazing, but I got a wife that's acting funny. And your man is trying to kill me, and I'm sitting her playing with fire," Savage said.

Jada sat up, showing her fat pussy, wide hips, and perfect breasts.

"Savage, my life is at risk. Zoe is connected. If he finds out I'm cheating on him with you, I'm dead, and my child is too. But I've loved you since I was a kid, I did," Jada said.

Savage thought Jada was crazy. This was why he stayed away from crazy bitches. He got dressed and headed for the door because he wasn't in the mood.

Jada stood there naked, with her arms crossed as she watched Savage walk out the door. It was as if her love was walking out of her life.

She never begged a nigga for sex, love, or money, but she wished she had a chance to tell him the bad news. Jada began to cry. But when she felt her stomach flip, she ran to the bathroom and started to vomit in the toilet.

Savage walked outside with many things his mind. As the cool breeze hit his Armani slacks, he felt as if someone was staring at him. So after he stopped and looked around, he hopped in his Range Rover, unaware of the all-black Camaro tailing him.

***

Lil Shooter had been laying low since the murders of the FBI Agents a couple of weeks ago. Lil Shooter and Lil Snoop had recently heard about Gangsta Ock's death and they weren't about to take it lightly. Both men were riding around in Lil Snoop's new all-white 600 Benz, listening to Kodak Black, and smoking a blunt of purple Kush.

Lil Snoop was riding around Jacksonville, reminiscing about his fallen soldiers, Dirty Red, Big S, Fresh, Trov, and even Gangsta Ock.

The two were on the hunt for any Yankees, even a Yankee hot, and Zoe Pound members. They always stuck out and in Dade County. They were everywhere.

"I swear, I'ma kill all of them niggas, folks," Lil Snoop said as he inhaled the loud.

"Bruh, where are you driving to?" Lil Shooter asked, wondering why he'd been driving around for an hour taking back roads.

"We about to pay respect to the homies. That's the least we can do," Lil Snoop said while giving him the evil eye.

Once they approached the gravesite from the secret dirt road, they pulled up behind a brand-new Lexus GS with rims. A passenger in it nodded his head to a Jim Jones song. They laughed until they saw a Yankees hat.

Stone came to visit his father's gravesite with Tango, but Stone had questions to ask his father, and he prayed for a sign.

"I'm sorry for this life. I could've did better but I wanted to be a boss. I could've went to the NBA, pops. I saw you at my high school and college games," Stone said with a smile.

"I needed you as a kid. My stepdad was a bitch nigga that looked down upon people like us," Stone said sadly.

"I'ma kill your murderer, even if it's the last thing I do," Stone said strongly.

"Well it may be the last thing in your next life," Lil Shooter said with a smile.

"Do what you do, blood, but let me die in dignity and honor," Stone said.

"I respect that, but pride is what kills us as a whole," Lil Shooter said as he blew Stone's brains onto his father headstone.

On the way back, Lil Shooter saw Fresh's grave, which read 1994-2014, and Dirty Red's grave, which read 1996-2014. Lil Shooter shook his head, thinking of how the youth was dying in these violent streets. He made it back to the car to see Lil Snoop doing something in the Lexus trunk.

Lil Shooter saw him chewing on something with ketchup on his face.

"What the fuck you doing, my nigga?" Lil Shooter said as he lifted the trunk up to see blood dripping from his lips. Lil Shooter saw Lil Snoop with a big knife in one hand and Tango's liver in the other hand.

"Leave his body in the truck and let's go," Lil Shooter said, pissed off.

Lil Snoop was Lil Shooter's cousin. He'd known he was crazy and needed help since they were kids. But the shit he'd just done was too much.

Chapter 25

Savage sat in his Palm Beach condo, playing Xbox with Lil Smoke.

"Where you been at Savage? I start daycare soon. Did you know that?" Lil Smoke said, pausing the Call of Duty game.

"Yes, I know, little man. I can't wait. And I been busy at work, trying make money so you can have all the toys in the world," Savage said.

"Big Sis is never here no more. It's just me and nanny. I miss y'all," Lil Smoke said sadly.

Savage wondered what Britt was up to because lately she had been avoiding him. As he started to ponder more on it, Britt walked into the condo with a slight attitude.

Savage got up and followed her into the kitchen to see what her issue was.

"Did I do anything to upset you, boo?" Savage asked.

"Nigga, what's wrong with me, you ask? No. what the fuck is wrong with you?" Britt said angrily.

"I'm stuck here while you run the streets and do God knows what. I had to drop out of college while you play tag in the streets," Britt said, holding back her tears.

Savage didn't know what to say because he'd been so busy fucking Jada and trying to find Big Zoe that he'd forgotten about his family.

"Britt, I'm sorry. Shit been crazy. I've been losing friends and I forgot about what really matters. Britt, I'm sorry. I got a lot on my mind."

"I'm going to the mosque to get back on my clean," Savage said as he grabbed his keys to his H2 Hummer.

Savage left Britt with glossy eyes and a mad face, while he ran out the door frustrated.

Savage called Big Art and told him to meet him at the mosque to make the Zhuru prayer.

After prayer, the two went into the office to talk business.

"I just got word that all of the New York fools are dead. I met up with Lil Snoop and they caught the nigga who shot you," Big Art said.

"Now let's focus on Zoe," Savage said.

"Lil Shooter said he gotta speak to you about Lil Snoop," Big Art said, opening his Qur'an.

"Okay, but I'ma talk to Jada tonight. It's time for Big Zoe to go," Savage said, thinking about how good her pussy was.

Both men exited the mosque, discussing details about Bama's appeal. While standing in front of the mosque, Savage felt like everyone was staring at him. Then, out of nowhere, a black van pulled up full of men dressed in all-black. They hopped out, busting shots in broad daylight.

Savage and Big Art started to shoot back, killing three men instantly. Big Art was chasing down one of the shooters until he felt a burn from his left side, which caused him to slow down.

Once Big Art saw blood leaking, he went crazy until his gun was empty. Then his body fell on the curb. Savage ran to help Art because he was out of bullets, and everybody was dead. Savage saw Big Art drop two more Zoe Pound members, who were coming from around a car, taking Savage by surprise. As soon as the gunmen were about to light Savage up with bullets, an all-black Camaro came rolling down the street with the windows halfway up pointing a 50cal out the window. The mystery driver killed the last two gunmen with headshots, and then sped off.

Savage was confused, but he had to get Big Art to a doctor. Thirteen Muslims came rushing out of the mosque to see dead bodies of their own members, and even kids. The only one still alive was Big Art, so the Muslims helped Savage put him in a pickup truck to take him to Dr. Abdulla's house. He was a licensed doctor that worked from his home.

A young Muslim took Savage and Big Art's empty guns, hopped in his hooptie, and pulled off before the pigs came. Once the pigs came, there were no witnesses, only dead bodies lying around with shells.

***

Bama finally made it to Miami's federal holding jail. His name was already heavy in the jail. The Savage crew was like the Supreme team in New York, but more violent. Bama's cellmate was from the Bronx, NY. His name was Smitty Da Don.

"Yo, Bama, did you see the news this morning, son? Niggas is brazy down here. I thought Brooklyn and Yonkers niggas was wild, shit," Smitty said, while doing Burpees in the cell.

"What happened?" Bama asked, reading his Qur'an.

"Shit, over eleven was murdered in front of a big mosque in a shootout, drug related, even two kids were killed," Smitty said, wiping sweat from his chiseled chest and abs.

"What was the mosque name?" Bama asked.

"I believe it was called Toque," Smitty said.

Bamma stopped reading because he knew it was Savage's mosque. He hoped and prayed his friend and Muslim brother was ok as he made wudo and prepared for the Asr prayer.

Smitty sat on the bunk while his celly prayed, thinking about how crazy the streets were everywhere, not in just New York. But Miami was like Iraq or Desert Storm.

After Bama prayed, he hopped in his Qur'an, trying to get peace of mind and trying not to think about the outside world, as most inmates do.

Chapter 26

Papi Goya was sitting in his conference room with his favorite black businessman, Savage, discussing plans, as usual, with the young man.

"I respect you, Savage, as a businessman and gentleman. You have a strong character. Most people lack in that area. That's why I requested this sit down today," Papi Goya said.

"I found out some disturbing news that may or may not be helpful to you. But a guy named Killer is in Mexico, dealing with the Mexican Cartel, and word is he put three million on your head," said Papi as he puffed on his Cuban cigar.

Savage's face said it all. His blood was boiling. He could taste blood, killer's blood at that, and he vowed to kill him.

"Savage, I am a very connected person, and the Mexican Cartel we're dealing with is powerful. Believe me, I used to be a boss. I'm not a person that plays two sides. I'm on your team because you've earned my loyalty, so I'm here for you," Papi Goya said.

Savage wanted to go to Mexico, but he knew his team wasn't strong enough to face the cartel at all. *But soon*, he thought.

"Thanks, Goya, for everything. But I will not put my problems in your hands. I owe you that much," Savage said as he stood to leave.

"No worries. Plus, me and Montana got some old business to attend to anyway," Papi said with a smirk.

***

Hours Later

Savage was in a low-key apartment he'd rented out in South Miami. He had plans to meet Jada there, instead of going to a hotel and risking being seen. He felt South Miami was the best location.

Once Jada arrived, he had plans to tell her it was over. But once she started deep throating his dick, while swallowing his cum, he was speechless and numb.

After almost sucking him to sleep, Jada went to the bathroom to wash her mouth out. She felt there was something really wrong with him. Plus, it had taken him an hour to cum on her face.

"Are you okay?" Jada asked as she laid in the bed, pussy wet and horny.

Before Savage could say it was over, Jada cut him off.

"Listen, Savage, I know I've been hard to deal with, but I need you now more than ever because I'm pregnant," Jada said, looking in his eyes.

Savage felt his heart drop. He thought she was speaking French.

"What the fuck you say?" Savage said.

Jada got a little nervous because his eyes bulged wide and his face turned red.

Savage relaxed because it was no way around it, and he refused to kill his seed, even though Britt wasn't going for this.

"Okay, I'm here for you, Jada. We going to make it work. I'ma take care of you and your other seed. Y'all can live here, fuck Zoe," Savage said, lying out loud. "Just respect my life, wife, and my family," Savage said, taking deep breaths.

Jada cried tears of happiness because she was his first baby's mother, unlike Big Zoe, who had eight other kids.

Jada got dressed and told Savage she was going to pack her shit and move in tonight. Savage walked in the kitchen and looked out the window in deep thought, wondering how his life had gotten so bad.

***

Savage arrived at his Palm Beach condo two hours later. Once he entered the condo, Ms. Jackson was sitting on the couch watching lifetime.

"Hey, Lil Smoke is sleep," Ms. Jackson whispered.

"Have you seen Britt?" Savage asked.

"No, honey, she been gone mostly all day," Ms. Jackson said.

Savage tried to call her, but it went straight to her voicemail, so he texted her to hit him ASAP.

Savage hoped she was safe but the thought of her cheating flooded his mind but he had guilty conscious he knew she was a good girl that's why he married her. He even felt like telling her everything but as fast as that though came it disappeared he knew Britt was still crazy. Savage had a plan to get rid of Jada once and for all it was his only move or he could lose his family. He sat in his room thinking of a way to end her life without anyone finding out it was him.

***

Jada was driving home listening to her favorite Darnell Jones album "Gemini" and thinking about her soon-to-be baby's father. Jada pulled up to Big Zoe's mansion, but before she exited her Maserati, she texted Savage, "I love you baby daddy."

Jada didn't see any security or none of Big Zoe's cars until she saw his white Lambo parked on the side. Jada ran in the house, unaware of the black Camaro parked across the street.

As soon as she walked in the house, she heard Big Zoe on the phone with another bitch, on speaker, saying how she couldn't wait to suck his balls.

Jada laughed to herself because she knew that would be the only thing she'd be sucking. His dick was stuck in his belly somewhere.

As soon as Big Zoe saw Jada, he hung up on Tamika, the stripper. Jada stood in front of him, shaking her head.

"Marqus, I can't do this no more, so I'm taking my son and we leaving," Jada said proudly.

Big Zoe laughed at her. Then he slapped the shit out of her, causing her to fall on the floor.

"Bitch, I tell you when to leave," Big Zoe said, cocking his hand back to slap her again. Then he heard a soft voice behind him.

"Naw, that's not how you hit a hoe, fat boy," Britt said. She was standing in his house, dressed in an all-black cat suit, showing only her pretty face and curves as she slowly walked towards them.

Big Zoe looked at the Lisa Ray lookalike, who was pointing two guns at him, in shock.

Jada almost pissed herself when she saw Britt. The fearful look on Jada's face made Big Zoe wonder what the fuck was going on.

"Who the fuck are you, bitch?" Big Zoe asked, laughing, and staring at her camel toe.

"I'm the devil," Britt said as she walked up to Big Zoe and started slapping him with the pistols until he was lying in a puddle of his own blood. Big Zoe was now teetering on the verge of consciousness. He wondered if it was a hit. Now he feared for his life.

Earlier in the day, Big Zoe had paid an assassin from overseas two million dollars to kill Savage and whoever was around him. But he never saw the killer in person. He'd dropped the money off in a car. Then he received a text saying the mission would be completed soon.

Big Zoe gave all his security the night off so he could make love to Jada and have peace and quiet. But he didn't know how Britt made it past the five K-9 dogs that were trained to kill.

Britt had enough of the cries from both of them, so she shot Big Zoe in the face six times with a bright smile, while walking towards Jada, who was hiding in the corner.

Britt was having so much fun. It was like a dog in heat for her.

"So you ruined my family, bitch. Fucked my husband, and thought you was safe. Bitch, you must be stupid," Britt said, knocking her in the face with her steel-toe boot.

Britt was now stomping on Jada's face like she stole something. In reality she did, she'd stolen her man.

"I saw everything, from y'all sex, the hotels, and the hours y'all spend together," Britt said through tears.

Jada was shaking her head, trying to deny it. But the more she moaned or cried, the more Britt stomped her, laughing.

"Bitch, this is your dead end," Britt said, putting a 357 in her mouth.

Jada tried to mumble something, but it was worthless because Britt fired two shots into her face, killing her instantly and spilling blood everywhere.

***

Days Later

Bama was in the court of appeals in front of Judge Romeo, dressed in an all-black Armani suit. He was watching his paid lawyer go in on his behalf, while staring at the ceiling in prayer.

"Judge, my client is innocent. The two agents who falsely arrested my client confirmed they played major parts in paying witnesses to lie. And the missing police reports from the crime scene should be more than enough to set my client free," Mr. Lawrence said.

"I have made my sincere decision," the Judge said. "The state of Florida and according to the federal constitution, I am going to…

To Be Continued…
Life of a Savage 3
Coming Soon

Submission Guideline

Submit the first three chapters of your completed manuscript to ldpsubmissions@gmail.com, subject line: Your book's title. The manuscript must be in a .doc file and sent as an attachment. Document should be in Times New Roman, double spaced and in size 12 font. Also, provide your synopsis and full contact information. If sending multiple submissions, they must each be in a separate email.

Have a story but no way to send it electronically? You can still submit to LDP/Ca$h Presents. Send in the first three chapters, written or typed, of your completed manuscript to:

LDP: Submissions Dept
Po Box 944
Stockbridge, Ga 30281

DO NOT send original manuscript. Must be a duplicate.

Provide your synopsis and a cover letter containing your full contact information.

Thanks for considering LDP and Ca$h Presents.

<u>Coming Soon from Lock Down Publications/Ca\$h Presents</u>

BOW DOWN TO MY GANGSTA

By **Ca\$h**

TORN BETWEEN TWO

By **Coffee**

THE STREETS STAINED MY SOUL **II**

By **Marcellus Allen**

BLOOD OF A BOSS **VI**

SHADOWS OF THE GAME II

By **Askari**

LOYAL TO THE GAME **IV**

By **T.J. & Jelissa**

A DOPEBOY'S PRAYER **II**

By **Eddie "Wolf" Lee**

IF LOVING YOU IS WRONG… **III**

By **Jelissa**

TRUE SAVAGE **VII**

MIDNIGHT CARTEL III

DOPE BOY MAGIC III

By **Chris Green**

BLAST FOR ME **III**

A SAVAGE DOPEBOY III

CUTTHROAT MAFIA II

By **Ghost**

A HUSTLER'S DECEIT III

KILL ZONE **II**

BAE BELONGS TO ME III

By **Aryanna**

CHAINED TO THE STREETS III

By **J-Blunt**

KING OF NEW YORK V

COKE KINGS IV

BORN HEARTLESS IV

By **T.J. Edwards**

GORILLAZ IN THE BAY V

TEARS OF A GANGSTA II

De'Kari

THE STREETS ARE CALLING II

Duquie Wilson

KINGPIN KILLAZ IV

STREET KINGS III

PAID IN BLOOD III

CARTEL KILLAZ IV

DOPE GODS II

Hood Rich

SINS OF A HUSTLA II

ASAD

TRIGGADALE III

Elijah R. Freeman

KINGZ OF THE GAME V

Playa Ray

SLAUGHTER GANG IV

RUTHLESS HEART IV

By Willie Slaughter

THE HEART OF A SAVAGE III

By Jibril Williams

FUK SHYT II

By Blakk Diamond

THE DOPEMAN'S BODYGAURD II

By Tranay Adams

TRAP GOD II

By Troublesome

YAYO III

A SHOOTER'S AMBITION III

By S. Allen

GHOST MOB

Stilloan Robinson

KINGPIN DREAMS II

By Paper Boi Rari

CREAM

By Yolanda Moore

SON OF A DOPE FIEND II

By Renta

FOREVER GANGSTA II

GLOCKS ON SATIN SHEETS II

By Adrian Dulan

LOYALTY AIN'T PROMISED II

By Keith Williams

THE PRICE YOU PAY FOR LOVE II

DOPE GIRL MAGIC II

By Destiny Skai

THE LIFE OF A HOOD STAR

By Rashia Wilson

TOE TAGZ III

By Ah'Million

CONFESSIONS OF A GANGSTA II

By Nicholas Lock

PAID IN KARMA III

By **Meesha**

I'M NOTHING WITHOUT HIS LOVE II

By Monet Dragun

CAUGHT UP IN THE LIFE II

By Robert Baptiste

NEW TO THE GAME II

By **Malik D. Rice**

Life of a Savage III

By **Romell Tukes**

Quiet Money II

By **Trai'Quan**

THE STREETS MADE ME II

By **Larry D. Wright**

Available Now

RESTRAINING ORDER **I & II**

By **CA$H & Coffee**

LOVE KNOWS NO BOUNDARIES **I II & III**

By **Coffee**

RAISED AS A GOON I, II, III & IV

BRED BY THE SLUMS I, II, III

BLAST FOR ME I & II

ROTTEN TO THE CORE I II III

A BRONX TALE I, II, III

DUFFEL BAG CARTEL I II III IV

HEARTLESS GOON I II III IV

A SAVAGE DOPEBOY I II

HEARTLESS GOON I II III

DRUG LORDS I II III

CUTTHROAT MAFIA

By **Ghost**

LAY IT DOWN **I & II**

LAST OF A DYING BREED

BLOOD STAINS OF A SHOTTA I & II III

By **Jamaica**

LOYAL TO THE GAME I II III

LIFE OF SIN I, II III

By **TJ & Jelissa**

BLOODY COMMAS I & II

SKI MASK CARTEL I II & III

KING OF NEW YORK I II,III IV

RISE TO POWER I II III

COKE KINGS I II III

BORN HEARTLESS I II III

By **T.J. Edwards**

IF LOVING HIM IS WRONG…I & II

LOVE ME EVEN WHEN IT HURTS I II III

By **Jelissa**

WHEN THE STREETS CLAP BACK I & II III

THE HEART OF A SAVAGE I II

By **Jibril Williams**

A DISTINGUISHED THUG STOLE MY HEART I II & III

LOVE SHOULDN'T HURT I II III IV

RENEGADE BOYS I II III IV

PAID IN KARMA I II

By **Meesha**

A GANGSTER'S CODE I &, II III

A GANGSTER'S SYN I II III

THE SAVAGE LIFE I II III

CHAINED TO THE STREETS I II

By **J-Blunt**

PUSH IT TO THE LIMIT

By **Bre' Hayes**

BLOOD OF A BOSS **I, II, III, IV, V**

SHADOWS OF THE GAME

By **Askari**

THE STREETS BLEED MURDER **I, II & III**

THE HEART OF A GANGSTA I II& III

By **Jerry Jackson**

CUM FOR ME I II III IV V

An **LDP Erotica Collaboration**

BRIDE OF A HUSTLA **I II & II**

THE FETTI GIRLS **I, II& III**

CORRUPTED BY A GANGSTA I, II III, IV

BLINDED BY HIS LOVE

THE PRICE YOU PAY FOR LOVE

DOPE GIRL MAGIC

By **Destiny Skai**

WHEN A GOOD GIRL GOES BAD

By **Adrienne**

THE COST OF LOYALTY I II III

By Kweli

A GANGSTER'S REVENGE **I II III & IV**

THE BOSS MAN'S DAUGHTERS I II III IV V

A SAVAGE LOVE **I & II**

BAE BELONGS TO ME I II

A HUSTLER'S DECEIT I, II, III

WHAT BAD BITCHES DO I, II, III

SOUL OF A MONSTER I II III

KILL ZONE

By **Aryanna**

A KINGPIN'S AMBITON

A KINGPIN'S AMBITION **II**

I MURDER FOR THE DOUGH

By **Ambitious**

TRUE SAVAGE I II III IV V VI

DOPE BOY MAGIC I, II

MIDNIGHT CARTEL I II

By **Chris Green**

A DOPEBOY'S PRAYER

By **Eddie "Wolf" Lee**

THE KING CARTEL **I, II & III**

By **Frank Gresham**

THESE NIGGAS AIN'T LOYAL **I, II & III**

By **Nikki Tee**

GANGSTA SHYT **I II &III**

By **CATO**

THE ULTIMATE BETRAYAL

By **Phoenix**

BOSS'N UP **I , II & III**

By **Royal Nicole**

I LOVE YOU TO DEATH

By Destiny J

I RIDE FOR MY HITTA

I STILL RIDE FOR MY HITTA

By **Misty Holt**

LOVE & CHASIN' PAPER

By **Qay Crockett**

TO DIE IN VAIN

SINS OF A HUSTLA

By **ASAD**

BROOKLYN HUSTLAZ

By **Boogsy Morina**

BROOKLYN ON LOCK I & II

By **Sonovia**

GANGSTA CITY

By **Teddy Duke**

A DRUG KING AND HIS DIAMOND I & II III

A DOPEMAN'S RICHES

HER MAN, MINE'S TOO I, II

CASH MONEY HO'S

By Nicole Goosby

TRAPHOUSE KING **I II & III**

KINGPIN KILLAZ I II III

STREET KINGS I II

PAID IN BLOOD **I II**

CARTEL KILLAZ I II III

DOPE GODS

By **Hood Rich**

LIPSTICK KILLAH **I, II, III**

CRIME OF PASSION I II & III

By **Mimi**

STEADY MOBBN' **I, II, III**

THE STREETS STAINED MY SOUL

By **Marcellus Allen**

WHO SHOT YA **I, II, III**

SON OF A DOPE FIEND

Renta

GORILLAZ IN THE BAY **I II III IV**

TEARS OF A GANGSTA

DE'KARI

TRIGGADALE I II

Elijah R. Freeman

GOD BLESS THE TRAPPERS I, II, III

THESE SCANDALOUS STREETS I, II, III

FEAR MY GANGSTA I, II, III

THESE STREETS DON'T LOVE NOBODY I, II

BURY ME A G I, II, III, IV, V

A GANGSTA'S EMPIRE I, II, III, IV

THE DOPEMAN'S BODYGAURD

Tranay Adams

THE STREETS ARE CALLING

Duquie Wilson

MARRIED TO A BOSS... I II III

By Destiny Skai & Chris Green

KINGZ OF THE GAME I II III IV

Playa Ray

SLAUGHTER GANG I II III

RUTHLESS HEART I II III

By Willie Slaughter

FUK SHYT

By Blakk Diamond

DON'T F#CK WITH MY HEART I II

By Linnea

ADDICTED TO THE DRAMA I II III

By Jamila

YAYO I II

A SHOOTER'S AMBITION I II

By S. Allen

TRAP GOD

By Troublesome

FOREVER GANGSTA

GLOCKS ON SATIN SHEETS

By Adrian Dulan

TOE TAGZ I II

By Ah'Million

KINGPIN DREAMS

By Paper Boi Rari

CONFESSIONS OF A GANGSTA

By Nicholas Lock

I'M NOTHING WITHOUT HIS LOVE

By Monet Dragun

CAUGHT UP IN THE LIFE

By Robert Baptiste

NEW TO THE GAME

By **Malik D. Rice**

Life of a Savage I II

By **Romell Tukes**

LOYALTY AIN'T PROMISED

By Keith Williams

Quiet Money

By **Trai'Quan**

THE STREETS MADE ME

By **Larry D. Wright**

<u>BOOKS BY LDP'S CEO, CA$H</u>

<u>TRUST IN NO MAN</u>

<u>TRUST IN NO MAN 2</u>

<u>TRUST IN NO MAN 3</u>

<u>BONDED BY BLOOD</u>

<u>SHORTY GOT A THUG</u>

<u>THUGS CRY</u>

<u>THUGS CRY 2</u>

<u>THUGS CRY 3</u>

<u>TRUST NO BITCH</u>

<u>TRUST NO BITCH 2</u>

<u>TRUST NO BITCH 3</u>

<u>TIL MY CASKET DROPS</u>

<u>RESTRAINING ORDER</u>

<u>RESTRAINING ORDER 2</u>

<u>IN LOVE WITH A CONVICT</u>

<u>Coming Soon</u>

BONDED BY BLOOD 2

BOW DOWN TO MY GANGSTA

Romell Tukes